"I Came To New Orleans To Find My Late Husband's Son, His Heir," Samantha Explained. "His Name Is Louis Dulac."

"I'm Louis DuLac," said the handsome mystery man with whom she'd just shared a night of incredible passion. His features grew hard and he gazed at her through narrowed eyes.

Sam's knees almost gave out. If he hadn't been holding her wrist she might have plunged backward down the stairs.

"But you can't be." The words fell from her lips, dazed and barely coherent. "It's impossible."

"Come in," he said. This time, it was a command rather than an invitation. He still held a firm grip on her wrist.

She felt herself struggling for breath. He tugged her toward him. "You're my late husband's…oh no." She tried to free herself.

He pulled her closer. "You're not going anywhere."

Dear Reader,

Young, beautiful women who marry rich, older men are often treated cruelly in the press. These "trophy wives" seem to be objects of intense fascination and resentment, as evidenced by the ghoulish obsession with Anna Nicole Smith after the passing of her wealthy older husband.

The coverage of her life and tragic death made me wonder how it would feel to be subject to such envy and loathing. It sparked the idea for *The Heir's Scandalous Affair,* in which young widow Samantha Hardcastle has to find her way in the world after the death of her billionaire husband, Tarrant.

With the eyes and cameras of the world upon her, Sam finds herself falling in love with the one man she should stay far, far away from: her husband's illegitimate son. I hope you enjoy Sam and Louis's roller coaster romance.

Jen

JENNIFER LEWIS

THE HEIR'S SCANDALOUS AFFAIR

Silhouette® Desire

Published by Silhouette Books

America's Publisher of Contemporary Romance

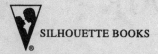

SILHOUETTE BOOKS

Recycling programs for this product may not exist in your area.

ISBN-13: 978-0-373-76938-4
ISBN-10:   0-373-76938-5

THE HEIR'S SCANDALOUS AFFAIR

Visit Silhouette Books at www.eHarlequin.com

Printed in U.S.A.

Books by Jennifer Lewis

Silhouette Desire

The Boss's Demand #1812
Seduced for the Inheritance #1830
Black Sheep Billionaire #1847
Prince of Midtown #1891
*Millionaire's Secret Seduction #1925
*In the Argentine's Bed #1931
*The Heir's Scandalous Affair #1938

*The Hardcastle Progeny

JENNIFER LEWIS

has been dreaming up stories for as long as she can remember and is thrilled to be able to share them with readers. She has lived on both sides of the Atlantic and worked in media and the arts before she grew bold enough to put pen to paper. Happily settled in New York with her family, she would love to hear from readers at jen@jen-lewis.com. Visit her Web site at www.jenlewis.com.

For my mother, who encouraged my love of books from the beginning, and who was my on-the-spot correspondent in New Orleans while I wrote this story.

Acknowledgment:

Thanks once again to the lovely people who read my book while I was writing it, including Amanda, Anne, Betty, Carol, Cynthia, Leeanne and Marie, and my agent Andrea.

One

Samantha Hardcastle was wound tighter than her late husband's Cartier watch. The festive happy-hour crowd on Bourbon Street jostled and bumped her. Her new red Christian Louboutin sandals were supposed to lift her spirits. Instead they threatened to bring her down on her butt.

She pushed through the throng toward a less crowded side street, gasping for oxygen in the beer-scented darkness. Streetlights and neon bar signs blurred and jumped in her peripheral vision. Columns holding up the balconies above clustered around her like menacing trees in an enchanted forest.

She was dizzy and light-headed. Probably because she'd forgotten to eat since…had she even had breakfast before her flight?

Her ankle wobbled and she caught herself on a brick wall. She'd somehow lost her way between the shoe store and the hotel. The sun had set, transforming the unfamiliar city into a place of shadows, and now she couldn't find her way back.

Since her husband's death, she couldn't seem to do anything right anymore. Every day took just a little bit more energy than she had.

"Are you okay?" a deep voice asked in her ear.

"Yes, fine, thanks," she responded. She didn't take her hand off the wall. The dark street was spinning.

"No, you're not. Come inside."

"No, really, I…" Visions of being taken captive fired her imagination as a thick arm slid around her waist. She struggled against hard muscle.

"It's just a bar. You can sit down and rest a minute."

He guided her to a doorway. A light-filled archway in the hot darkness. A soothing string instrument filled the air, which—strangely enough—didn't smell of beer like the air outside.

"There's a comfortable chair over here." His tone was authoritative, yet soothing. The large room had the atmosphere of a turn-of-the-century saloon. Ornate gilding, polished plank floors and high tin ceilings. The colors were muted and mellow. Restful.

She let herself be helped to a leather armchair in a dark corner of the bar. "Thanks," she murmured, as he lowered her gently into the chair. "I don't know what came over me."

"Just rest. I'll bring you something to eat."

"But I don't—"

"Yes, you do."

She thought she detected a hint of humor in his firm rebuttal. Maybe she did need food. She kept forgetting to eat lately. She'd totally lost her appetite for—everything.

She glanced around. There were quite a few people sitting at tables and in booths along one wall. Unlike the jovial mob outside, they spoke in hushed tones, and their laughter tinkled in the air.

Two waiters set down a table in front of her armchair, crisp white cloth and gleaming flatware already on it. A strong hand brought a steaming white plate.

"Here, crawfish étouffée with dirty rice. Just what the doctor ordered."

"Thank you." She glanced up at the owner of the hand and the reassuring voice. "You're too kind."

"Oh, I'm not kind at all." Honey-brown eyes glittered with humor. "I don't like people passing out cold in front of my door. Bad for business."

"I guess dragging dizzy women in is one way to drum up customers." She risked a shy smile.

He smiled back with warmth that surprised her. He had chiseled features and tousled dark hair and was far too good-looking to be trustworthy.

Apprehension trickled up her spine. "Why are you staring at me like that?"

"I'm waiting for you to pick up your fork and eat."

"Oh." She grabbed the fork and scooped up a small mouthful of étouffée. Self-conscious under his penetrating gaze, she put it between her lips and attempted to chew. Flavor cascaded over her tongue as she bit into the tender crustacean, marinated in its spicy sauce.

"Oh, my. That's good."

A smile spread over his stern features. He gestured for her to continue. "Now, what can I get you to drink?"

He asked the question with a hint of seduction. Not like a waiter, more like…someone trying to pick her up in a bar.

A hackle slid up inside her. She'd dreaded being single again. Dreaded it with every cell in her body.

"Just a glass of water will be fine, thank you." She spoke in a clipped and officious manner. Like the wealthy Park Avenue matron she supposedly was.

He vanished out of her line of sight. With a sigh of relief, she fell on her crawfish étouffée, ravenous. She'd been walking around all day, trying to locate the man she hoped was her husband's estranged son.

She'd finally found Louis DuLac's house on Royal Street, with its tall windows and scrolled iron balconies. But he wasn't home. She'd tried twice.

The second time his housekeeper had shut the door rather firmly in her face.

Some festival was in full swing and the city was packed with tourists. She'd overlooked that when she arranged her trip. Her husband's private jet didn't require reservations, and the ten-thousand-dollar-a-night rooms were still available. It wasn't Mardi Gras, though. She knew that was in February or March, and right now it was October.

A loud pop made her look up. Champagne streamed over the side of a Krug bottle. Apparently Mr. Smooth had pegged her as the kind of person who could afford seven hundred dollars a bottle.

Probably her own fault. The red Louboutin shoes didn't help.

"Oh, I really don't—"

"On the house," he murmured, as he filled a tall, fluted glass.

She blinked. Even Tarrant's favorite sommeliers didn't hand over Krug champagne for free. "Why?"

"Because you're too pretty to look so sad."

"Does it occur to you I might have good reason to look sad?"

"It does." He handed her the glass and pulled up a chair. "Are you dying?"

There wasn't a hint of humor in his gaze.

"No," she blurted. "At least not that I know of."

Relief smoothed his brow. "Well, that's good news. Let's drink to it." He'd filled himself a glass and he raised it to hers.

She clinked it and took a sip. The expensive bubbles tickled her tongue. "What would you have said if I'd told you I was dying?"

"I'd have suggested you live each day as if it's your last." His eyes sparkled. They were an appealing caramel color, with flecks of gold, like polished tigereye. "Which I think is good advice in any event."

"You're so right." She sighed. Her husband, Tarrant, had such a lust for life that he'd far outlived his doctor's expectations. She'd vowed to follow his example, but wasn't doing very well so far.

Drinking champagne was a start. "Here's to the first day of the rest of our lives." She raised her glass with a smile.

"May each day be a celebration." His eyes rested on hers as he raised his glass. She felt a strange flicker of something inside her. A pleasurable feeling.

Must be the champagne.

"Do you see the guitarist?" He gestured to a corner of the room. "He's one-hundred-and-one years old."

Samantha's eyes widened. The musician's white hair contrasted starkly with his ebony skin. It was astonishing he even had hair at that age. And his spirit shone in his energetic finger movements that vibrated out into the air as music.

"He's lived through two world wars, the depression, the digitization of almost everything and Hurricane Katrina. Every day he plays the guitar. Says it reignites the fire in him every single time."

"I envy him his passion."

"You don't have one?" He cocked his head slightly. His gaze was warm, not accusatory.

"Not really." She certainly wasn't going to tell this stranger about her quest to find her husband's missing children. Even her closest friends thought she was nuts. "Shopping for shoes sometimes lifts my spirits." She flashed a smile and her new red Louboutins.

In a way, she hoped he'd sneer. That would squash the funny warm sensation in the pit of her belly.

Instead, he smiled. "Christian is an artist and art always lifts the spirits. He'd thoroughly approve."

"You know him?"

He nodded. "I lived in Paris for years. I still spend a lot of time there."

"I'm impressed that you could tell who designed a pair of shoes. Most men wouldn't have a clue."

"I've always had an appreciation for fine things." His gaze rested lightly on her face. Not sexual or suggestive, but she couldn't help but hear the words *like you* hover in the air.

Instead of feeling harassed she felt…desirable. Something she hadn't felt in a long time.

She brushed the feeling away. "Is New Orleans always this crazy?"

"Absolutely." He grinned. "Some people who come here have such a good time they even forget to eat." He glanced at her almost-empty plate of crawfish and rice.

She smiled. Let him think she was here for a fun vacation. In another life, maybe she would have been. Tarrant had loved jazz and they'd talked about coming for the spring Jazz Festival.

"Don't go looking sad again." He shot her an accusatory glance. "I think you need to dance."

She glanced over his shoulder where a cluster of elegant couples swayed on the dance floor. Adrenaline trickled through her.

"Oh, no. I couldn't." She took a quick sip of champagne. She was a widow. In mourning, though she'd promised Tarrant she wouldn't wear black even to the funeral. She flashed her shoes as an excuse.

He tilted his head and narrowed his eyes. "Christian would be horrified if he heard a woman had used his shoes as a reason not to dance."

"Then don't tell him."

"I most certainly shall tell him—unless you dance with me. I think it's the least you can do after I rescued you from the streets and fed you." A smile played around his mouth.

She chuckled. "You make me sound like a stray waif."

"A stray waif in Christian Louboutin shoes." He stood and extended his arm. Apparently he expected her to rise, too.

She took his hand and stood. She was nothing if not polite, the society-wife training ensured that. Besides, what was wrong with one little dance? Tarrant would rather see her moving than moping around.

He made a signal to the guitarist, who winked and struck up a new tune. Bluesy, but with a Latin flavor. Sam felt a shimmer of excitement as they stepped out onto the smooth wood floor. She hadn't danced in a long time.

The music hovered around them like smoke, filling the space between them. Through the sensual mist it created, she couldn't help but notice her partner was tall and broad shouldered. Her eyes were about level with his shirt collar, which had a fine pattern of irregular stripes. His jaw was solid, authoritative, like the rest of him.

He took her hand and clasped it softly, wrapping long,

strong fingers around hers. The warmth of his blood seemed to pulse through his skin and heat hers as the music beat around them.

"What kind of dance are we going to do?" She didn't dare look up at his face. Already she was too close to him. So near she could feel the heat of him through her clothes.

"Any kind you like. It sounds like a mambo to me."

Her feet slipped into the mambo rhythm, following the patterns she'd learned years ago at Ms. Valentine's dancing school. She tried to focus on the steps, on moving gracefully, and keeping enough distance between her and her partner. He smelled of spices, like the rich food she'd eaten, and of starched cotton.

"I like your shirt." She risked a glance at his face.

Those rich, honey-colored eyes gazed at her, twinkling with amusement. "You don't have to make polite conversation with me. I know you're nice."

"How on earth would you know that?"

"I can read people. It's a gift I got from my grandmother. She used to read tea leaves, but she told me her secret was always to read the people as they stared at the leaves."

"What do you look for?" She tried to ignore the steady warmth of his big hand on her back.

"Facial expression tells you what matters to someone, not just while you look at them, but every day. All the little dimples and wrinkles reveal something."

"Uh, oh. I'm getting self-conscious." Two plastic surgery consultations had reassured her that it wasn't yet time to get drastic, but at thirty-one, Samantha knew she was no longer at the peak of her once-prize-winning beauty.

"That dimple in your chin tells me you smile a lot. And the tilt of your eyes tells me that you like to make people happy."

"That's true." She let out a nervous laugh. "I've been told I try too hard to please. I'm a 'yes' woman."

"But you have strength of character. I can see that by the way you carry yourself. You care very much about everything you do."

She frowned, taking in his words. Was it true? Maybe she just had good posture from training for beauty pageants.

She'd tried hard to mature. To learn from her failed marriages and all the mistakes she'd made.

She'd given everything she had to make Tarrant's last years the best they could be.

"And you're very, very sad." His low voice tickled her ear. While they moved, he'd come closer.

"I'm okay," she stammered, trying to reassure herself as much as him.

"You are okay." His hand shifted on her back, stroking her. "You're more than okay. But my grandmother would tell you to breathe."

"I am breathing," she protested.

"Little shallow breaths." He leaned into her. She could feel his hot breath on her neck. "Just enough to keep you afloat, to get you through the day."

He squeezed her hand inside his. His penetrating gaze almost stole the last of her breath. "You need to inhale and draw oxygen way down deep into your body. To let it flow all the way through you, out to your fingers and toes."

Her toes tingled. "Right now?"

She swallowed. Glanced around his broad arm to where other couples danced, lost in their own world.

"No time like the present." He smiled.

He had a nice smile, warm and friendly. She might not be a tea-leaf expert, but she was no slouch at reading people, either. A survival mechanism she'd learned early on in her volatile household.

Of course, he was still far too good-looking. No man grew to adulthood with looks like that without an outsized and highly chiseled ego to match.

"Go on, breathe."

Their feet had been keeping time to the music, but suddenly he stopped. Holding her with one arm around her back, and one hand on hers, he waited for her to follow his command.

Aware that their nonmovement must be attracting attention, she sucked in a breath. Her breasts lifted several inches inside the thin, white dress before she blew it out, blushing.

"Nice try, but you need to draw it down into your chest." He tapped her back with his fingertips. "All the way down to my fingers."

She glanced over her shoulder.

"Breathing's not a crime in this state." He grinned. "Come on, let's do it together. One, two, three…" Eyes fixed on hers, he drew a breath deep into his chest, which swelled under his shirt.

Sam tried her best to match the length and duration of his breath. When she finally blew it out, she was gasping. "How embarrassing."

"Not at all. That was great. You'd be surprised how many people go through life every day holding their breath without realizing. You don't want to do that." He flashed a grin and swept her into the mambo rhythm again. Twirled her fast and tight until she had to suck in a breath just to keep her balance.

"You want to breathe it all in, everything, the good and the bad."

"The bad?"

"If you try too hard to avoid the bad stuff, you end up missing out on the good stuff, too." His narrowed eyes shone like a cat's in the dim interior. She tried to ignore a little tug in her belly.

Was it all the deep breathing? She couldn't tell, but something had changed.

Their dance became more intense as he pulled her closer, whipped her out and then drew her back in. A drummer had joined the guitarist on stage and the hypnotic, pounding rhythm of palms on bongos pulsed through her until her feet took on a life of their own.

She found herself moving faster, deeper, throwing herself into the dance. She drew air deep into her lungs as she whirled through the air, and came back to rest against his hard body. Somehow everything was effortless, flowing, and she found herself losing track of which part of the room they were in.

The drumming grew louder, then faded away, the clinking of glasses blended with the rhythmic strumming of the guitar, until the whole atmosphere seemed to throb, to breathe, in and out, round and round.

Sam laughed aloud with sheer delight. When the music stopped with a flourish, she fell into her partner's arms. "That was fantastic."

"You're an incredible dancer."

"I'm a very rusty dancer, but you're onto something with that breathing."

"In and out, that's all it takes."

"It's funny how we forget the little things that are most important."

He made another hand signal to the guitarist, who launched into a slow song with cascades of rippling notes. Sam let her body sway instinctively to the seductive sound.

The club's interior was warm and she could feel her skin— glowing, to put it delicately, but she wasn't embarrassed.

Her partner's reassuring gaze rested on her eyes, not probing or poking about the rest of her the way so many men did.

Without even thinking, she inhaled deeply and blew it out, and enjoyed the smile that stretched across his handsome face.

I don't know his name.

How odd. To be dancing with someone and have no idea who he was. She knew he owned the bar, so he had an identity, but without a name he wasn't quite…real.

Should she ask?

She blinked, strangely reluctant. A name seemed so formal, like a passport or driver's license that gave you official status. She didn't want to tell him that she was Samantha Hardcastle. Her name and picture might not ring any bells down here in New Orleans, but in New York they'd been plastered over the papers for months.

The Merry Widow, with her much older husband's billions now at her disposal. Like she'd *won* or something.

Bile rose in her gut. She didn't want this man to know anything about that. To form preconceptions about her as a gold-digging tramp who married a rich man for his money.

"Hey, you okay?" His hand slid around her back.

She realized her breathing had grown shallow again. She swallowed. "Sure, I'm fine. Sorry!" She drew in a deep and deliberate breath for his benefit, and they both chuckled as she blew it out.

The guitarist, joined by a saxophonist, as well as the drummer, launched into a swinging, bluesy number. His eyes were closed and his head bobbed in time with the music as if he were captivated by its spell.

Sam let that spell guide her feet as they danced without

touching, their bodies swaying to the rhythm. Sensual and muscular in his movements, her partner moved with effortless ease.

Maybe it was the sips of champagne, but Sam felt strangely weightless, like all her cares and worries had drifted up to the ornate tin ceiling and hovered there, leaving her free and light.

"Were you a professional dancer?" His breath warmed her neck as he leaned in.

She colored slightly. "I competed a few times. Does my dancing look too artificial?"

He shook his head, his smile reassuring. "Not artificial, just polished, like the rest of you."

She resisted the urge to glance down. She couldn't deny being polished. As Tarrant's wife, it had been her job. Her hours in between social lunches and dinners were filled with appointments to get her nails tipped or her hair trimmed.

She was so used to being buffed to a high shine that she had no idea what she'd look like without the carefully highlighted hair and couture dresses. If she stripped all the expensive enhancements away, would there be anyone there at all?

Right now it didn't matter. Her partner's expression shone with quiet appreciation. That honey-brown gaze didn't seem to accuse her or to find anything lacking.

She couldn't help but notice the way his hips moved. How they linked to strong thighs just visible beneath the smooth surface of his dark pants, to his flat belly.

A young, athletic body in the peak of health. A beautiful thing.

How old was he? Early thirties probably. Her age, though most of the time she felt about ninety.

He picked up her left hand and examined it. It felt very

naked without the big engagement and wedding ring Tarrant had given her with such fanfare only four years ago.

The engagement ring had a diamond too big to wear outside without an armed guard. The wedding ring had been buried with his coffin. Tarrant had wanted her to place it on his hand like Jackie Kennedy did when her famous husband died. He always enjoyed a dramatic flourish.

"You're smiling." His deep voice stirred something in her chest.

"Happy memories." How odd to have that as a happy memory. She was getting pretty strange in her old age.

"Now you're not smiling." He tugged her hand and pulled her closer. "I think you need to step outside your memories and into the present."

He slid his arm around her waist. Her breasts crushed gently against his chest and a warm surge of pleasure rippled through her.

"I love this song," he murmured. His low timbre vibrated in her ear, sending a shiver along her spine. "It makes me think of a lazy day out on the bayou. Sun shining on the water, cranes watching from the trees, the *putt-putt* of a shrimp boat in the distance."

The image formed in her mind, a peaceful scene, at odds with their rather urbane surroundings. "Do you go there much?"

"As often as I can."

She couldn't see his face because he'd pulled her too close. His arms wrapped around her waist and she found that hers had slipped around his neck. A quick glance confirmed that other couples danced the same way, wrapped up in each other, to the gentle strumming of the guitar and the low caress of the saxophone.

He lowered his cheek to hers and she felt the slight stubble

on his chin. A delicious masculine sensation she'd almost forgotten.

Almost, but not quite. The familiar strains of desire echoed through her like the notes of the music. It stirred in the palms of her hands where they pressed against his broad shoulder blades, in her nipples as they bumped his hard chest, in her tongue, which wondered what his mouth would taste like.

The answer came as their lips touched, opened, and her tongue flicked over his. His sensual mouth was both soft and firm, his tongue at first tentative, then insistent, hungry.

Her fingers dug into the crisp cotton of his shirt. Her belly pressed against his firm hips, as she tilted into the powerful kiss.

Light and color crackled behind her eyelids, dazzling her, while their tongues danced together. Then, slowly, their tongues drew back, and his lips closed. She felt his warm skin part from hers, to be replaced by cool, air-conditioned air.

Still clutching his back, she opened her eyes and blinked in the dim light. Her breath came in unsteady gasps, her legs wobbled and her skin stung with arousal.

"Come with me." He didn't look at her and it wasn't a question. With one arm firmly about her waist, he led her off the floor and across the room. Faces and bodies blurred around her as she tried to get her bearings.

I only had two or three sips of champagne. The thought flickered through her mind then flew away on a low note from the saxophone. Under her flimsy dress, her body pulsed and throbbed, and if he wasn't holding her up, she wasn't sure she'd still be walking.

Maybe she'd be floating.

They left the crowded restaurant through a door behind the bar that led out into a dim hallway. Across the hall he opened a tall, polished wood door. "More private."

He ushered her into a beautiful room, decorated in the same prohibition-era style as the bar, as if Woodrow Wilson might wander in and start arguing with Franklin D. Roosevelt. Antiques gleamed in the soft light from a beautiful glass light fixture. The interlacing pattern of stained glass was so harmonious and unusual that she wondered aloud, "Is that a Tiffany lamp?"

"Yes, my mother collects them."

Her eyes widened. "Aren't they worth hundreds of thousands of dollars?"

He shrugged and opened a wood cabinet. "What use are beautiful things if you can't enjoy them?" He pulled out two crystal glasses and another bottle of Krug champagne.

"You do enjoy the good life, don't you?"

"I consider myself privileged to have the opportunity to enjoy the good life. I'd be a fool to squander it."

Sam smiled as he offered her the bubbling glass. "Do you live here?"

"No, this is more like…my office."

"It's lovely." She glanced around. Was there a bedroom?

And was it good or bad if there was?

"It's unchanged since 1933, when the original owner was shot dead by his lover."

Sam gasped. "Why'd she shoot him?"

"He slept with his wife."

She laughed. "I can see how a mistress would find that offensive."

Already they'd crossed the room and entered a large, high-ceilinged chamber with a grand, four-poster bed. Rich gold draperies glowed in the light from another jewel-toned Tiffany lamp.

He lifted the arm of an old Victrola phonograph and placed

it on the record. The mellow tones of a big band orchestra swelled from the brass horn.

His sensual gaze rested on her mouth. "I love your smile."

"Thanks, I love it, too. I haven't used it enough lately."

His eyes fixed on hers for a second, stalling her breath. Her lips buzzed with sensation. Had she really kissed him?

He stepped toward her and placed his glass on the polished sideboard.

Her insides trembled with long-forgotten desire. Anticipation mingled with fear as she watched his mouth, watched his eyes caress her body with their soft gaze.

Was he going to kiss her again?

Her answer came as his lips closed over hers in a swift motion that stole her breath.

Louis DuLac had kissed a lot of women.

He'd run his fingers over a lot of smooth skin and stared into a lot of desire-darkened eyes.

But this was a first.

He'd never met a woman whose every glance and movement resonated with passion and intensity that threatened to make sparks in the air.

She was blond and blue-eyed, his mystery woman, not so unusual.

She was slight, frail even, her limbs so thin his grandmother would have pinched them, clucked, and brought her some food.

Which, of course, is pretty much what he did.

"Why are you smiling?" Her mouth was pink from kissing, pursed with slight shyness.

"You'd be smiling, too, if you enjoyed this view."

She lay naked, half hidden under the crisp sheets, her body

softly illuminated in the ruby glow of a nearby lamp. Small, high breasts gave her a girlish aspect, but the far distance he glimpsed in her eyes spoke of a thousand lifetimes lived.

He almost regretted bringing her here.

Almost.

Her rosy nipple thickened between his thumb and finger. Her heart beat visibly just below her rib cage, and he saw its pace pick up as he trailed his fingers down toward the triangle of golden hair at the apex of her thighs, which writhed under their thin cover.

Her arousal was palpable, a primal hunger crouching below the surface. He could see it in the glitter of her dark pupils, in the silver sheen of her skin. He could taste it in the hunger of her kiss and feel it in the heat pulsing through her slender limbs.

The scent of her drove him half-crazy. Some expensive French concoction, no doubt, but mingled with the fresh, clean smell of her skin and hair, it was perfect.

Louis flicked his practiced tongue over her sensitive nerve endings and, through narrowed eyes, watched her hips buck slightly.

He deepened his exploration with fingers and tongue. Her fine gold hair splayed on the pillow and her eyes slid closed as she gave herself over to sensation. He was gratified to see her draw deep, unhurried breaths while he pleasured her.

Her fingertips roved into his hair and along his neck as he licked her until her hips shuddered. Then he stopped and pulled back.

Her eyes flicked open in—dismay? He smiled. "No hurry. We have all night."

Or did they? He had no idea if she had somewhere to be. Someone to meet.

No wedding band. He'd checked. That didn't mean much these days, but it reduced the chance of him ending up like the bar's original owner.

She raised herself up on her elbows, eyes shining. "I want to kiss you." Her voice was soft and sweet, her request so simple and innocent, it belied the fact that she'd removed her clothes with the candor of a practiced call girl.

She certainly wasn't that.

But she was a mystery.

One moment shy and awkward, the next polished and witty. Dressed in her fine clothes, she reeked of wealth and privilege. But the Louboutin shoes and John Galliano dress didn't hide the ragged emotional edge of a hungry waif. You didn't have to be psychic to see she was burdened with a sadness so huge that it threatened to suck oxygen from the air.

He shouldn't have brought her here.

She was too fragile, too slender and delicate, too dangerously close to some verge he knew nothing about.

He had a strange feeling that, in unlocking her mysteries, he'd open a Pandora's box that would unleash chaos on his world.

But he couldn't stop.

Two

Sam awoke with a start.

She blinked, searching for the familiar night-light in her room, but finding only blackness. A brush of warm skin against her elbow reassured her that she slept next to her husband…

Her husband was dead.

She sat up, heart pounding. Images plucked at her mind: flashing honey-gold eyes, strong and sensuous hands, a wickedly seductive smile.

The sound of breathing was just audible in the thick darkness. She heard a car drive by outside. Why was it so quiet?

She was in New Orleans. In a strange man's bed.

Her breath caught in her throat. Her thighs were sticky and her insides still pulsed with the stray echoes of arousal.

She'd *made love* with this man lying beside her.

She didn't even know his name, or anything about him, but she'd stripped naked and dived into his bed like a…like a…

Her eyes had adjusted to the point where she could make out the shapes of furniture in the thin moonlight sneaking through a crack in the heavy drapes. She eased herself to the edge of the bed, dipped her legs over the side and felt for the floor.

Cool wood on the soles of her feet shocked her more fully awake.

What was she thinking?

She wasn't thinking, that was the problem. At least he didn't know who she was. Or she hoped he didn't.

She could see the headlines already. *Gold-Digging Tramp Back on the Prowl.*

Of course they wouldn't be far wrong. Her husband was dead less than six months, and already she was naked in the arms of a handsome stranger.

Was she insane? Like, really, truly crazy?

She'd had her doubts lately, but this was different.

Fear propelled her into action. She glanced back at the bed and saw the shape of him outlined by white sheets, still apparently asleep. She needed to get out of here before he woke up.

Heart thundering and pain lancing her temples, she groped around for her clothes. Luckily, since she'd removed them herself, she knew they were on a chair near the bed. She struggled into her underwear, then slid the dress over her head.

Carrying her sandals in her hand, she crept toward the looming dark outline of the door.

She didn't feel crazy. She felt dangerously sane, as she turned the ornate brass knob with painstaking care not to make even a single click. She pulled back on the heavy wood door, praying that it wouldn't creak.

A glance over her shoulder reassured her that he was still asleep.

Her lover.

Her hand shook on the door when she remembered the feel of his hands on her skin. How gentle his touch was, how careful, and then how hungry and naked and…human she'd felt in his arms.

She hadn't felt like that in a long time.

Sam swallowed hard and stepped over the threshold. She closed the door behind her with the same agonizing slowness. She wasn't sure whether to be relieved or sad when it slid into place without even a click, and she left her handsome stranger behind, still deep in dreamland.

Was he dreaming about her?

She walked over an air-conditioning register, and the cool breeze shot up her dress. Her aroused flesh tingled and her nipples tightened. Shimmers of awareness still crept over her skin.

The sensation of intense arousal was raw and uncomfortable. Unfamiliar and unsettling. An unsteady ache settled in her chest.

She picked her way carefully across the floor, avoiding the fine old furniture and priceless lamps.

Almost there. But relief didn't come even as she released a heavy bolt and opened the door to the hallway. First, she'd be leaving this man's door unlocked, which, in a city with a high crime rate, might have any number of consequences.

But that wasn't it.

There was an uglier word for what she'd done.

Betrayal.

She'd betrayed her husband. Betrayed her vows to him and all the promises she'd made before and after. She'd betrayed her purpose here in New Orleans, which was to find his missing son and heir and bring him home to the family.

And she'd betrayed herself. She'd prided herself on her stoicism. On her steady attention to duty and the fact that she wasn't a foolish girl anymore.

Only to find out tonight that in fact she was so "easy"—or desperate—that she'd go home with the first man to gaze into her eyes.

She snuck along the empty corridor, through a heavy, bolted door, and into the silent bar. There must be another way out, but she didn't want to take the time to find it.

She tiptoed through the cavernous space, so recently filled with sensual music and laughter, now empty and silent.

Accusatory.

Long shadows chased her across the floor as a car drove by outside. She found herself ducking like a criminal, and crawling the rest of the way to the door.

Shame soaked through her. What had brought her to this? She'd thought herself older and wiser and better able to avoid the mistakes she'd made in the past.

The latch on the door was old and heavy, with an unfamiliar mechanism. She struggled with it for a full five minutes, silent sobs rising in her throat, before finally the bolt slid free and she was able to tug the door open.

She waited until the next block to put her shoes on. Even then the pathetic clickety-click of the narrow heels made her feel like a target.

No one around. If they were, she was easy prey in her foolishly thin dress and high heels, clutching her expensive purse with far too much cash in it.

Would she find her way back to the hotel and her normal life? Or would she spend eternity wandering the dark, humid streets of a strange city?

She probably deserved the latter.

* * *

Still too sleepy to open his eyes, Louis reached out his hand, anticipating contact with warm silky flesh. His fingers found nothing but cold sheets.

His eyes flicked open. Empty sheets.

Louis tried to shake off the sensual fog that had followed him from sleep. He'd dreamed about her. In his dream, she'd been laughing, throwing her head back with abandon, eyes sparkling in the sun.

He propped himself up on one elbow and scanned the room. Her clothes were gone.

He sank back into the sheets, disappointment blooming in his chest.

Not a surprise that she'd vanished, his woman of mystery. For a moment he even wondered if he'd simply imagined her.

She'd never told him her name, or where she was from. He hadn't asked, mostly because he didn't think she'd tell him, anyway.

They'd had a wonderful night—no expectations, no obligations, no tearful goodbyes, just a few hours of intense pleasure.

He'd probably never see her again. Which should be fine.

Except that, for reasons he couldn't put his finger on, it wasn't.

Sam patted her hair and inhaled deeply as she approached the gates of Louis DuLac's beautiful French Quarter house for the third time. She'd reached unconsciously for the big gold ring on her middle finger. Tarrant had given it to her for their first anniversary, and she never went anywhere without it. For some reason, she'd forgotten to wear it last night. She'd forgotten almost everything else, too—propriety, duty, common sense. Only a few brief hours ago she'd been in bed with a total stranger.

She inhaled deeply as she stepped under wrought-iron balconies and reached for the bell.

She was here in New Orleans to find her husband's un-
claimed son and bring him into the family, and she couldn't
let a personal mistake interfere with that goal. Besides, last
night was a silly indiscretion born of painful loneliness, and
she was going to forgive herself for it.

An old-fashioned chime sounded inside the house. Her
heart thudded as she prayed he'd be home. She didn't want
to be turned away yet again and no one ever returned her calls.

No sound reached her from the other side of the door. Apparently even the maid was out today. She rang again. This
time she heard feet coming downstairs. A voice talking.
"…the terms were good, but the property needs to be com-
pletely renovated and if we're going to open in time for the
season, I just don't have the time to…hold on."

Something about the voice sounded vaguely familiar, even
through the heavy, black-painted door. Her scalp prickled
with awareness.

A very uncomfortable awareness.

The door flew open and shock snapped through her as she
stood face-to-face with the man from last night.

Bright morning sunlight illuminated his unmistakable chiseled features and glittered in his golden-brown eyes. Recog-
nition lit his features and a smile started across his mouth.
"Hold on," he said again into the phone.

"I—I—I'm sorry, there's been a mistake," she stammered,
stepping backward.

"Come in." He stood aside and gestured for her to enter.
She peered past him into a dim, cool hallway with a large,
ornate mirror on one wall.

"No, I—I can't. I didn't mean to—" Her mind froze, and

she found herself backing away, glancing over her shoulder so as not to fall down the steps.

"I'll call you back," he muttered into the phone. He lunged forward and grabbed her wrist. His strong fingers closed around her arm. Her muscles tightened as she instinctively resisted.

He held her firm. "Don't think you can ring my doorbell then run out on me *again*."

Guilt seared her. She had sneaked out of his room without saying goodbye. He must be angry.

But humor glittered in his gaze. "How did you know where I live? We never even exchanged names. I think the least you could do is introduce yourself."

Sam's mind whirled. "I—I'm Samantha Hardcastle."

The smile faded from his eyes. "What?"

"Samantha Hardcastle, I came here to find my husband's son. His name is Louis DuLac and this must be the wrong address so I'm not sure what happened, but—"

"It's not the wrong address." His features grew hard and he gazed at her through narrowed eyes. "I'm Louis DuLac."

Sam's knees almost gave out. If he hadn't been holding her wrist she might have plunged backward down the stairs.

"But you can't be." The words fell from her lips, dazed and barely coherent. "It's impossible."

"Impossible or not, it's a fact. Come in."

This time his words were a command rather than an invitation. He still held a firm grip on her wrist.

"Oh, boy." Sam felt herself struggling for breath. He tugged her, gently, and she stepped toward him. "You're my husband's...oh, no." Her heart sank right down in her chest as her rib cage closed around it like a fist.

"I confess I don't know exactly what's going on here, but

this time I plan to get to the bottom of it." He studied her face with a slight frown. "You're not going anywhere until you come in and tell me what's going on."

Sam gulped. Her body was screaming at her to turn and run—to save herself—but her brain struggled to behave in a more civilized manner. She put one foot in front of the other and moved toward the doorway.

He didn't let go of her wrist until she'd stepped inside the threshold and he'd closed the door behind her.

"You're Louis DuLac?" The surprise in her voice seemed to amuse him.

"Have been since the day I was born."

"Maybe there's another Louis DuLac. It could be quite a common name."

He turned. Crossed his arms over his chest. He wore a pale blue shirt with crisp cuffs and collar. "I know who you are, Samantha Hardcastle. I've been ignoring your letters and phone calls for months."

Sam inhaled. "Why?"

"Why don't you come up to my office and we'll talk."

"I really don't think I should."

"Don't worry, I won't tear your clothes off." He gazed at her through narrowed eyes.

Was that mischief or malice that glittered in their depths?

Sam felt her face redden. She'd torn her own clothes off last night, if she remembered correctly. She deserved his scorn.

"It's up one floor." He led the way up a wide, polished stair-case with an elaborate carved handrail.

The cool air-conditioned interior contrasted starkly with the already hot and humid morning air outside. Fine antiques decorated the large space in a minimalist and appealingly modern fashion. A pleasant smell of lavender enhanced the calm and ordered atmosphere.

"Do you live alone?" Her question popped out before she could consider its implications.

He turned, frowning. "Yes, in case you're worried that I was cheating on my wife last night, let me reassure you that I am single and unattached with no existing obligations."

"That's not what I meant." Or was it? Her pulse jackhammered under her skin. "I was just wondering."

"Wonder away. Curiosity's no crime." A mischievous half smile slid across his mouth for a split second, then vanished. "My study. Please come in."

Sam walked past him into a large, high-ceilinged room with a massive walnut desk at its center. The walls were painted sky-blue, topped by ornate white cornices that hung like clouds near the ceiling. "This is a spectacular house."

"Thanks. I inherited it from my grandparents. I've been fixing it up room by room." He glanced at the chiseled cornice with obvious pride.

Then his attention snapped back to her. "Please, take a seat." His accusatory gaze undermined the smooth politeness of his request.

"And why don't you tell me *exactly* what you're doing here?"

Louis leaned back in his armchair, wove his fingers together and rested them on the desk. The blonde had some explaining to do.

First, she'd driven him half-wild in bed, then snuck out in the middle of the night without a by-your-leave.

Second, she was apparently the crackpot sending him all these strange messages about a long-lost father wanting to welcome him back to his bosom.

She balanced precariously on the edge of her chair, pulse

visible at her slender throat, light wisps of hair fluttering in the breeze from the air-conditioning.

Nervous. As well she should be.

She twisted a big gold ring on one of her long, elegantly manicured fingers. "I came here to find you. To New Orleans, I mean. You haven't returned my calls or letters."

"And you thought it might be a good idea to sleep with me first?" He couldn't figure that part out.

"I had no idea who you were!" A flush of color spread from her sharp collarbone up her neck. "I didn't intend to sleep with anyone, least of all…" She swallowed hard.

Your stepson?

His mind boggled. "What makes you think I'm your husband's son?"

"*Late* husband. He died six months ago." Grief, still sharp, was evident in the suddenly taut lines of her face.

Pity surged through him. "I'm sorry."

"When he found out he was dying, we decided to try and find the children he'd fathered. We hired a researcher and gave her all the information he had. We then tracked down the individuals indicated in the research and administered DNA tests to see if they really were related. We found his sons Dominic and Amado this way."

"And how did your research lead to me?"

"Your mother is Bijou DuLac."

"I am aware of that, yes."

"She had an affair with Tarrant—my late husband—in the winter of 1977."

"In Paris?" His mother had lived in Paris since 1969.

"In New York. She was visiting the city for a series of concerts. They spent a month together, then she moved back to Paris. According to our researcher, she gave birth to a son exactly eight months later. We believe you're that son."

Something hot and uncomfortable slid down his spine.

"I am my mother's only child, so if she had a son, it's me." He couldn't keep the edge out of his voice.

Who were these people sitting in offices analyzing his existence?

He'd never known who his father was and he'd gotten along just fine without that knowledge. He certainly didn't need someone shoving a parent—a dead one, at that—down his throat now that he was long past needing one.

He cocked his head. "My mother told me I was born of the chance meeting between a double bass and a saxophone."

Samantha Hardcastle blinked. "Which one was she?"

He laughed. "I don't know. She didn't say."

Her expression softened and the sparkle in her eyes reminded him of how she'd looked last night. Beautiful. So feminine and alive.

Right now she wore a cool, mint-green dress with short sleeves and a scooped neck. Fresh and edible as a mint julep.

He leaned toward her. "I don't know if I'm the person you're looking for, but I'm glad that your search brought you back. It was rude of you to sneak out without a goodbye kiss."

Maybe he'd hoped to see a pretty flush of color light her cheeks, or a flutter of remorseful eyelashes. Instead, the shine left her eyes and her mouth tightened.

"I'm so sorry." She looked down, twisting her hands in her lap. "I don't know what to say. What a terrible thing. It should never have happened."

Her voice shook and he saw her hands tremble. He wanted to take her in his arms.

But she'd just told him that the night she'd spent in his bed was regrettable.

He wanted to be mad, but she looked like she was about to cry.

"You're lucky my feelings aren't easily hurt." He managed to keep his tone light. "Women don't usually look back on a night in my bed like they screwed up and spent a night in jail."

"I had no idea who you were." She stared at him, blue eyes wide and brimming with tears.

"You still have no idea who I am. We didn't do all that much talking. But I'll start. I was born in Paris and grew up both there and here in New Orleans. I own six five-star restaurants and when the mood is right I play a little guitar." He narrowed his eyes. "But maybe you did know all that?"

She gulped. "All except the guitar."

"Thing is, I don't know anything at all about you. Maybe we should correct that."

She drew in a shaky breath, which had the unfortunate effect of filling the bodice of her minty dress with her perky breasts. His pants grew tight.

"Have you heard of Tarrant Hardcastle?"

"Of course. I've eaten at The Moon in New York. It even inspired the name of my newest restaurant."

"La Ronde," she murmured.

"You have done your research."

"It's supposed to be the best new restaurant in New Orleans."

"In the world," he challenged.

Still no smile.

"I'm…I was his third wife. He has a daughter from a previous marriage, but after he was diagnosed with cancer, he told me about a woman who'd tried to sue him for paternity decades ago. He said he'd been wondering about the child—a boy—and what happened to him. Once he got a sense of his own mortality, I think he became obsessed with finding an heir."

"His daughter wasn't good enough?"

"She's young, and probably not cut out for running a

luxury retail empire. God knows I'm not cut out for it, either, so I encouraged him to begin the search. Then he recalled other incidents—such as his affair with your mother—and we began to suspect that he might have a whole network of heirs out there."

"How encouraging."

"Don't judge him too harshly."

"I can't judge him at all. Apparently I'm no better than he is, though at least we used a condom, so we didn't make any heirs."

She blinked rapidly and color flooded her cheeks. "I'm so ashamed. Honestly, I can't even wrap my mind about it. That I slept with my husband's son." Her throat dried on the last word and it came out as a strangled sob.

"Calm down. For all we know I'm the result of a different one of my mother's many lovers. Let's not kid ourselves that we live in a kind of world where people mate for life, like swans."

Sam hesitated, probably taken aback by his bluntness. "Did your mother ever marry?"

"No. She said slavery was over and she wasn't going to chain herself to a man for any reason, ever."

Her pretty blue eyes widened. "She sounds like a character."

"She was a very unconventional mother, let's put it that way. She showed me how to live my life without being cramped by other people's expectations."

She nodded, looking thoughtful.

"So, a little thing like accidentally sleeping with my step-mother doesn't put a hitch in my stride."

Her mouth flew open, then snapped shut.

"But as we've already established, we don't actually know if you're my stepmother or not, so why don't we just assume you're not." He wove his fingers together and mastered his features in a pleasant smile.

"Will you take a DNA test?" The words rushed out.

Louis hesitated, his flesh crawled at the thought of someone spreading his genes out on a laboratory table and delving into them in search of whatever mysterious information was hidden there.

His father. Sure, he'd wondered who he came from. Was someone out there, walking around, with the same unusual eye color or with his feeling for music or his passion for food?

As a kid, being hustled from one country to another and allowed to do things most parents would never permit, he'd dreamed of a traditional father who'd pat him on the head and be there for him no matter what.

Mercifully, he got over it.

"Why take a test now? What good would that do? If the man you think is my father is already dead, there's no point." He narrowed his eyes. "Unless you're planning to snap off a chunk of the Hardcastle empire and hand it to me on a gold platter."

Her face was strangely impassive. Was that part of the plan?

"And you can shelve that idea because I've already made all the money I'll ever need and I have my hands full with my six restaurants and coaching the Little League team."

"Will you take the test anyway?"

Her question, deadly serious, knocked him off-kilter.

"Why? What does it matter if I'm his son or not?"

"Maybe it doesn't matter, maybe it does." She shrugged her slim shoulders inside her mint-green dress. Her calm voice was thoroughly undermined by the intense look in her eyes. It mattered to *her*.

"Maybe it would make you feel better if I take the test and

we can determine that I'm not your stepson." He found the whole thing rather funny. Maybe the situation was just too ludicrous to take seriously. What in the world was his supposed father doing married to a woman young enough to be his daughter, anyway?

"There's a lab a few blocks away. We could walk over there right now. It's totally painless and only takes a minute. They swab a few cells from inside your mouth."

"Something tells me you're not going to quit until I agree."

A smile tugged at her pretty mouth. "Just say yes."

DNA. A father.

He sucked in a breath. The prospect of actually knowing who his father was sent prickles of energy dancing along his nerves.

Family came with obligations, expectations. People could disappoint or could let you down. "What if I prefer being rootless and freewheeling?"

"Taking a test won't change that." She'd already picked up her clutch purse off the floor. Apparently, she'd declared victory and was ready to head for the lab.

His pride and some other even more primal instinct fought back. "I'll think about it." He cocked his head. "Maybe we could discuss it some more over dinner tonight. Have you eaten at my restaurant, La Ronde?"

She swallowed. "I don't think that's a good idea."

"You think I might seduce you again?" He lifted a brow.

Her cheeks paled.

Ouch.

"Or maybe you're worried you might seduce me."

"I'm beginning to think I have no idea what I might do, so I'd better barricade myself in my hotel room and hope for the best." She managed a bright smile.

"It might be more fun if you barricade me in there with you."

She shot him a warning look. "Please take the test. You won't regret it."

The plea in her eyes won him over.

At that moment, he decided to take her damn test. For reasons he didn't care to examine, he wanted to make the lovely Samantha Hardcastle happy. Something about her snuck right under his skin and grabbed him where it hurt.

He'd take her test and if he did regret it, it wouldn't be the first or last regret of his life.

Still, he wasn't going to give up his DNA without the promise of a second date. "You join me for dinner, I'll take your test. Deal?"

She blinked. Her mouth moved, but no words came out. She looked panic-stricken.

Louis didn't like the nasty feeling in his gut that came from a woman apparently desperate enough to refuse a fine dinner with him at his own five-star restaurant. "The food's good."

"I'm sure it is."

"And the company's all right, too."

She swallowed. Twisted her big ring. Suddenly she stood. "I have to go. Do you have a number where I can reach you?"

He scribbled his cell number on a piece of monogrammed notepaper. A warm sense of satisfaction and anticipation crept through him. Her resistance had only inflamed his desire.

She'd call. And she'd eat dinner with him.

And as far as he was concerned, that was just the beginning.

Three

Samantha dived out Louis DuLac's front door into the street. Thank heaven she didn't have a car waiting, because she needed to walk. Tension strung her muscles tight and vibrated along her nerves.

So, she'd found Tarrant's missing son.

And slept with him.

Shame soaked through her like acid. Part of her wanted to fly back to New York and never see Louis DuLac again.

But then she'd have failed everyone. Dominic, Tarrant's first son, was thrilled that a world-class restaurateur might be his brother.

Dominic had owned his own chain of gourmet markets before joining Hardcastle Enterprises. His newfound half brother Amado owned a fine vineyard. Just by dint of his occupation, they were sure Louis would turn out to be one of Tarrant's sons.

Fiona, Tarrant's daughter, had exclaimed that she traveled to Milan at least once a year to shop and always ate at Louis DuLac's restaurant there.

They'd all been excited about her trip down here to find him. And she'd promised Tarrant.

She drew in a long breath of sticky, humid air. Why did Louis have to insist on dinner as a condition for taking the test?

Then again, why not? If he were her stepson, it would no doubt be the first of many family dinners she hoped to enjoy.

Unless she'd destroyed that possibility forever with her foolish behavior last night.

Maybe she could get him to promise that they'd never mention their indiscretion to anyone.

It would be their secret that he'd run his lips over her skin until it tingled with arousal. That he'd kissed her breathless and whispered erotic suggestions in her ear. That he'd licked and sucked her almost to the point of madness, then made love to her until she cried out with joy.

Her skin heated and her insides roiled with an agonizing jumble of passion and humiliation.

She marched along Royal Street, not sure where she was going. Adrenaline crackled through her, propelling her feet forward.

She turned a corner, then edged around a crowd gathered to listen to a sidewalk guitarist.

The bluesy music combined with the hot air, the sounds of laughter and a spicy food smell wafting from somewhere turned the whole city into an exotic cocktail of temptation.

What next?

As she stood waiting to cross the street, a sign in a window opposite her caught her eye.

Need advice? asked the scrolled letters, painted on a white board. *Madame Ayida ~ Palmistry and spiritual consultations.*

Yeah, that's just what I need, Sam muttered sarcastically under her breath. Yet the sign arrested her gaze. The simple black letters beckoned her to look closer.

She paused and frowned.

She did need advice. Should she take Louis up on his offer of dinner in exchange for the DNA test? Or should she run back to New York with her tail between her legs and forget she ever met him?

She stared at the sign from the opposite sidewalk.

Could it hurt to ask?

She checked for traffic and crossed the road, and her legs seemed to march to the door of their own accord. Next she was turning the brass handle.

If talking to yourself was the first sign of madness, surely asking someone called Madame Ayida for advice was the second.

Nevertheless, Sam stepped through the door into a small, curtained foyer. "Hello," she called. "Anyone here?"

"Madame Ayida is always ready to help you," came a voice from the far side of the curtain. Black velvet, as clichéd as the name. Probably Madame Ayida was taking a break from the rigors of touring with the circus.

The curtain lifted and Sam found herself staring into a pair of dark brown eyes. "Please, come in and sit down."

Sam obeyed. Instead of the mole-covered crone she'd anticipated, Madame Ayida was young, with milk-chocolate-colored skin and a wide smile. A yellow silk scarf covered her hair in a strangely reassuring fairground touch.

"I don't really know why I'm here." Sam followed the garbled words with a breathy laugh.

"That is not unusual," said Madame Ayida. She had a slight accent, but Sam couldn't put her finger on it. "Together we will discover the reason for your visit."

Sam lowered herself gingerly into the single gold-painted chair opposite Madame Ayida at a small, wood table with a scarred top and scuffed legs. "So, um, do you read my palm, or what?" She glanced around. There was no sign of a crystal ball or tarot cards.

"If you like." Madame Ayida smiled enigmatically.

Sam held out her hand, suddenly embarrassed by her shiny manicure and big gold ring.

Madame Ayida closed soft fingers around her hand and lifted it for examination. Sam's heart fluttered in the long silence.

"A long life, but not without heartache," murmured Madame Ayida at last, her gaze lowered.

"That's for sure." Sam tried to keep her tone light. "Twice divorced and once widowed. Please, tell me it gets better."

Madame Ayida looked up, compassion in her eyes. "You're at a crossroad." She lowered her lashes, studying Sam's palm. "There's a risk that you'll make a terrible mistake."

An image of Louis's naked body, glistening with a sheen of perspiration, flashed into her mind. "I think I might have already made it."

"No." Madame Ayida shook her head slowly. "You're facing a choice and you haven't made it yet."

Sam's throat tightened.

Madame Ayida looked down at her hand, her forehead puckered with worry. "A difficult decision. I see a familiar road and one that is strange."

Sam frowned. There wasn't any sign of familiar roads in her life right now. If there was, she'd put her foot on it right away.

"Neither will be easy." Madame Ayida smoothed a forefinger over Sam's lifeline.

"Oh, great. Story of my life." Sam forced a laugh. "Then I guess it doesn't matter much which way I go."

"Oh, it does." Madame Ayida's eyes fixed on hers, dark pupils wide in the dim light. She seemed to look right through Sam and into some other realm beyond. "This choice will determine the course of the rest of your life."

"No pressure, then." Sam stared at her palm. It was hard to even make out the lines in the gloomy storefront. Probably Madame Ayida was making this up off the top of her head.

Those wide, intense eyes refocused and stared directly at Sam, making her breath catch at the bottom of her lungs.

"You *must* follow your heart."

Sam shivered, which was strange since the room must be at least eighty-five degrees.

Something in Madame Ayida's voice reached right into her mind and echoed there.

But how could she follow her heart when she wasn't even sure she could find all the broken pieces?

Tarrant's death had left her feeling so empty and cold. Sometimes she felt like her future had shriveled up and died with him.

"You belong with the living, not with the dead." Madame Ayida's soft voice penetrated her consciousness.

Sam blinked, startled. Had this strange young woman read her thoughts? "This terrible mistake you spoke of, how can I avoid it?"

"Listen to your heart." Madame Ayida's soft fingers palpated her palm for a second, as if Sam's heart might be found there and resuscitated.

Her blood pumped so hard she could almost hear it.

She had the chance to bring another member of Tarrant's family home to meet his siblings. Would her terrible mistake be squandering that opportunity just to salvage her own pride?

What was left of her heart pounded in her chest. It seemed to beg her not to blow the chance to bring Louis into the family.

At that moment, she decided to accept his invitation to dinner.

She'd find out if he really was Tarrant's son, and if he was, she'd start over and form a new relationship with him.

One with absolutely no hot, steamy, sweaty sex involved.

She realized she was staring into space. "Thank you. You've helped me a lot."

Madame Ayida smiled enigmatically. "Twenty dollars."

Sam fumbled in her purse. She was a grown-up. She could handle this. She could put that one accidental night behind her and start over, just as she'd started her life over after each of her failed marriages.

She certainly wasn't going to make the mistake of falling into bed again with a man who might be her stepson. She didn't have to worry about that.

Did she?

She pushed out into the blinding sunlight with a fresh sense of resolve. Madame Ayida might or might not be a rip-off artist, but she'd helped Sam organize her own thoughts, which was probably all these fortune-tellers ever did anyway.

She snapped open her phone, fumbled in her purse for the paper with Louis DuLac's number on it and dialed with shaking fingers.

His deep greeting made her throat dry, but she managed to blurt out, "I'll go to dinner with you."

She could hear his smile widen in the silence.

"Great. I'll pick you up at six."

"I'm at the Delacorte."

"I know."

"Oh." Sam frowned, then decided she really didn't want to know how he knew. She could wear the black Chanel dress with the white trim. That was probably the closest her wardrobe came to resembling a nun's habit. "Just so you know, we're not going to…uh…do anything, okay?"

It didn't make sense, but she could swear she heard silent laughter. "I promise we won't do anything you don't want to. I can be a perfect gentleman, when I try."

Sam heaved a shaky sigh. "Good." Still, fears nagged at her. "No touching. Like, not even to shake hands."

"Don't trust yourself, huh?"

"Not really." She swallowed and tried not to picture the light shining in those honey-gold eyes.

Better not to touch at all. You never knew what could happen.

Or rather she had some pretty vivid memories of exactly what could happen.

"Well, you can relax. I'll take good care of you. Be sure to wear something you don't mind getting dirty."

"What?" Her question was greeted by the steady sound of a dial tone. Dirty? Weren't they going to La Ronde? Unless it was under construction, she couldn't imagine how you could get dirty there. Unless maybe lobster was involved. With a lot of butter.

She closed her phone and put it back into her purse. Maybe not the Chanel, then.

Sam was already in the dim, quiet lobby of the hotel, seated in a leather chair with her eyes on the door, when Louis arrived. Her skin pricked with a mixture of fear and anticipation. Part of her was terrified to even be in the same room with him.

Another part of her was gloriously relieved to see him again.

She hadn't blown it. Yet.

There was still a chance to welcome him into the Hardcastle family. As her son. And she was just fine with that.

Or at least she would be if that's how things worked out.

She rose from the chair, smoothing wrinkles from her hastily purchased Calvin Klein pantsuit. She'd tried for casual elegance, so she'd look okay if they went to a restaurant or if they…

"Hi, Sam." A wide, warm smile lit up his face. His caramel-colored eyes shone with good humor.

He approached with long, easy strides, as if he intended to put his arm around her and kiss her on the cheek. The way one normally would.

But he slammed to a halt about a foot from her like he'd hit an invisible wall. His smile morphed into a wicked, challenging grin. "See?"

His hands hung by his sides. For a split second, her body ached at the lack of touch.

She bit her lip. "Hi, Louis."

"You decided to take a chance on dinner."

Sam glanced around, to make sure no one was in earshot. "I came here with a purpose, and I'm trying to get back on track."

He studied her for a moment. "Sometimes it's a good idea to get off the track and reassess."

Sam shook her head. "Some days it's all I can do to put one foot in front of the other. A track is reassuring for me right now."

He nodded slightly. "I won't derail you."

The golden glitter in his eyes contradicted his reassuring message. But that was probably just her overactive imagination.

"So, where are we going?" She glanced at his clothes. Khakis and a button-down shirt. Neutral, conservative attire. Yet somehow on him the generic outfit looked strangely hip and...

No. Not sexy. She was not at all aware of this man's sex appeal. Besides, the loose-cut cotton totally concealed the thick, strong muscles of his arms and chest. And his powerful thighs. She could see a hint of his slim waist and flat belly, but really, she wasn't at all interested.

She sucked in a breath. "Shall we get going?"

Louis held out his arm to take hers, then whipped it back as if stung. "Follow me," he murmured.

He was taking this no-touching thing seriously. Good.

Sam nursed her untouched arm. She'd instinctively lifted it an inch or two and it hung there in midair for a moment before she plastered it back to her side.

Excellent. Much better this way. She held her chin high as she marched out of the hotel lobby two steps behind him.

He pulled open the passenger door of a sleek, pale-yellow, open-topped sports car parked next to the sidewalk outside. He stood aside, so as to avoid any accidental brushing of skin, while she climbed in and sat on the tan glove-leather seat.

"What a beautiful Jaguar. How old is it?" Sam stroked the polished dashboard. Maybe she just needed to touch *something*.

"It's a 1967 XKE. It belonged to my grandfather."

"And it still runs?"

"It was his baby. He saved her for special occasions, and I do the same." He flashed her a golden glance before walking around to the driver's side.

A special occasion. "Where are we going?"

He settled behind the sporty wheel. "You'll see. Just sit back and enjoy the ride."

Sam fumbled with her seat belt, and tried not to notice that her nipples were almost painfully sensitive as she brought the strap over them.

Deep breath. Remain calm. Keep focused on your goal.

She snuck a glance sideways to see if he looked like Tarrant. Maybe he wasn't Tarrant's son at all?

But on close inspection, she could see Tarrant's determined jaw. His high cheekbones. The lofty carriage of a man with limitless confidence.

She sank into her seat, her breath shallow. How had she not noticed last night?

Louis's features were more generous, his mouth wider and quicker to smile than Tarrant's. His eyes were a totally different color with a more catlike shape. And his smooth olive skin made a mockery of the freckly tan that Tarrant so painstakingly cultivated to hide his natural pallor.

There was no avoiding the fact that Louis DuLac was a breathtakingly handsome man.

What a terrible shame Tarrant would never meet him.

A rush of emotion threatened to get the better of her and she reached into her pocket for a tissue.

"You okay?"

"I was just thinking how it's awful that you'll never meet your father."

"I don't know who my father is."

The admission didn't seem to faze him at all. Louis DuLac was obviously comfortable with himself, and didn't need to cling to anyone else for support.

She wished she had that kind of strength.

"And you don't know who my father is, either," he continued. He shot her a bright smile. "Does it matter? I'm the same person either way."

"You don't want to know, do you?"

"Not really."

"What are you afraid of?" She stared at him, trying not to admire the sculpted perfection of his cheekbone.

"Afraid?" He flashed an aggressive glance at her and laughed. "I'm not afraid of anything."

"I don't believe you. You must be afraid of something. Snakes? Spiders? The dark?"

"Three of my favorite things." A smile settled over his mouth as he watched the road. The city streets had leafed out into a lush suburb.

"Then you have nothing to lose by learning who your father is." She smiled and tossed her hair.

He'd backed himself into a corner.

"You're tricky." He shot a glance at her.

"I'm smarter than I look."

"You certainly always look very smart. Didn't I tell you to dress casual?"

"This is casual. It's Calvin Klein." She raised an eyebrow.

"Did you buy it today?"

"I might have. Or I might have had it for years." She crossed her arms over her chest. "Don't flatter yourself that I bought it to impress you."

"That wouldn't flatter me at all. I don't want to be impressed." He kept his gaze on the road.

"What do you want?" Nothing like getting to the bottom of things. Especially since there was no touching involved.

Though, maybe she was flattering herself by thinking he wanted to touch her again.

"I want you to be yourself. Take it easy. Feel the wind in your hair."

Be yourself? If only she knew who that was. She'd grown so used to trying to please everyone else she wasn't sure who was in there under all the smiles and smart outfits.

Time for a diversionary tactic. "Where are we going?"

"My very favorite place."

Louis decided not to tell her that his favorite place was well-stocked with snakes and spiders, and that it was most magical after dark.

He glanced sideways at Sam. Fresh and pretty, her pale gold hair tossed in the breeze. She didn't fuss over it and try to fix it like some women. He liked that.

"You're looking more relaxed already."

"It's beautiful here."

They'd left the city limits and headed out into the bayou on Belle Chasse. The air was warm and Sam had taken off her jacket. The wind pressed her textured cotton top to her skin, tracing her girlish curves.

It was okay to look, as long as he didn't touch.

Louis felt a bit like a kid in a toy store who'd already spent his whole allowance. He could look at all the pretty, shiny things, but he couldn't take them home.

At least not yet.

"Just last night, you were naked in my arms."

She swung her head around to look at him. Panic shone in her eyes. "I've never done that before."

"Had sex?" He raised an eyebrow. Couldn't resist teasing.

She shot him a scolding look. "Had sex with a man I just met."

"I hope it was a memorable first." He glanced at the road,

reluctant to take his eyes off her face. "I'll certainly never forget it."

Her neck turned pink. A very pretty pink that made him want to layer kisses over it.

She didn't say anything.

"A guy could feel quite rejected by your silence."

She flicked her hair back. "I did say we weren't going to do anything tonight."

"And we're not. No touching at all." He slid his fingers over the wheel, as if taking out his desire to fondle on the punched chestnut leather. "But no one said anything about no reminiscing. That was a beautiful night."

"I don't know what came over me last night," she said, her words slow and careful. "But I do know that it won't happen again."

As they drew close to the shed where he kept his boat, Louis wondered what on earth he was thinking when he came up with the crazy idea of bringing her here.

This was his special place. His sanctuary away from all the drama and intrigue of his everyday world.

The mysterious Samantha had closed up like a snail pulling into its shell. She wasn't rude, exactly, but his questions about her life were met with brief, colorless answers that told him nothing about her.

She was going to hate it here. There weren't any boutiques or musicians or celebrities and her high heels would sink into the wet ground. He should have taken her to La Ronde, as she'd expected.

Or not taken her anywhere at all, as she'd have clearly preferred.

"Where are we?" She peered around when they pulled up in front of the boathouse.

"The middle of nowhere." He jumped out of the car. The air was clear and cooler already, the sun sinking below the shiny, wet horizon. "Are you nervous?"

"It does occur to me that I know very little about you." She glanced around. He saw her notice that the road ended only a hundred yards or so away.

The boat shed was the only structure visible among the messy web of canals and grassy land that stretched out as far as the eye could see.

She opened her car door. "But you've got an honest face."

He laughed. "That's a first."

She stepped out onto the road. "Is this where we're having dinner?" Doubt hovered around the edges of her question.

"We've got a little farther to go, but we're bringing dinner with us." He unlatched the XKE's tiny trunk and pulled out the wicker picnic basket. His friends teased him for not using a plastic Igloo ice chest that would actually keep the champagne cold, but both his lovely old car and this beautiful woman deserved a bit more style than that.

She smiled. "A picnic."

"Is that okay?"

"I haven't had a picnic in…I don't know when I last had a picnic."

Maybe almost as long ago as you last had sex.

He didn't say it. But she had bottled-up fire and hunger inside her that must have taken years to accumulate. Maybe she'd never even had sex with her late husband.

The man she believed to be his father.

"We're going out on my boat." He ushered her into the dim, cool boat shed, restored and painted to look just as it had when his great-grandfather first erected it to house his beloved shrimp boat.

Louis's handmade reproduction of the old Lafitte skiff rested lightly on its rails, polished wood shining in the sunset glow that snuck in through the open doors out to the water.

Samantha's silence made him glance sideways. She stood, frowning at the boat. "I can't swim."

"You won't have to. This boat is the smoothest ride ever made and there's not a wave to be found on these waters."

Fear glimmered in her eyes. He wanted to put his arm around her and reassure her. To whisper that he'd take great care of her and he wouldn't let anything hurt or even scare her.

But he'd promised no touching.

"If you're not comfortable on the boat, we'll come right back. We can always eat in here."

Samantha bit her lip, a girlish gesture. "No." She sucked in a breath. "I'd like to go on the boat. I'm trying to step outside my comfort zone more often."

"An admirable thing to do." He held out his hand to take hers. She looked at it, then up at him.

He dropped his hand to his side. It prickled with the frustrated desire to touch her. "Old habits die hard."

He managed to resist offering to help her into the boat. She climbed on while it was mounted on the rails, then he removed his shoes, lowered the boat and its precious cargo gently into the water and climbed in himself.

Sam laughed at his soaked pants. "You're all wet."

"I'll dry. It's refreshing. You can go for a dip if you like."

She glanced over the rim of the boat into the dark, glittering water. "No, thanks. I don't want to go that far outside my comfort zone. Is it deep?"

"Not very. A lot of this was solid ground a few years ago. The water levels keep rising. Every year I'm closer to owning oceanfront property."

"This is nicer than the ocean. It's so quiet. And I love the sound the grasses make, like they're whispering secrets to each other." Her blue eyes shone with pleasure.

Louis felt a knot form in his gut. This was *exactly* why he'd brought her here.

Already he could see the tension slipping out of her shoulders and her hands spreading out over the wood gunwale as she relaxed into the boat.

The late afternoon sun shone on her skin and picked out flecks of sparkling gold in her hair.

Momentarily sorry that it would drown out the gossip of the grasses, he started the engine and guided the boat into a wide canal, where water shimmered among the grasses on either side. "You could open the basket for us."

She unlatched the leather buckle and reached in. "Goodness, what beautiful dishes. Are they silver?"

"My great-great-grandfather was a silversmith. I like them for picnics because they don't break."

She nodded, a smile flicking across her lips. "Tarrant would approve."

Louis's shoulders tightened at the mention of the strange man's name. "He liked nice things?"

"Only the best." She picked up a plate and he felt a familiar flash of pride as she traced the intricately carved pattern with her fingertip.

"I guess that's why he chose you." The words slipped out. He wasn't looking to flatter her.

She blushed. "I don't know why he chose me at all. We met at a party I was catering. It was my first night on the job and I spilled white wine all over his pant leg. The other caterers were sure the firm would never be hired again. They got me in such a panic that, when he asked me out while I was mopping him up, I didn't dare say no."

"A Cinderella story."

She laughed. "Yeah. I guess it was. I didn't have a penny to my name at the time because my second husband wouldn't let me take anything with me when I walked out."

"That's not too nice."

"He wasn't. That's why I left." She shrugged. "Best thing I ever did. Well, after leaving my first husband."

"He was a rat, too?"

"Most definitely. Ooh, is this potato salad?" She'd pulled the lid off a crock and dipped her nose down to inhale.

He watched her one tiny dimple deepen at the whiff of Creole mustard. "Great Aunt Emmeline's recipe."

"You have a lot of relatives."

"Maybe that's why I'm not looking to find any more."

She gave a little pout. She knew he wasn't serious.

"There's a spoon in the bottom, help yourself. And there's some andouille sausage in the warmer, and fresh rolls. And champagne, of course, in case we get thirsty."

Samantha eyed the champagne and flashed him a nervous glance. "I think I'd better stay away from that."

"You're afraid you might decide it's okay to touch me after all?" He leaned in, so close he could smell her lovely smooth skin and the natural feminine scent hiding under her elegant perfume.

"No." She spoke too quickly and he heard a ripple of hesitation in her voice.

The uncertainty hung in the air like smoke.

He felt it creep into his lungs and spread throughout his body as the image of her naked in his bed—just last night—flashed across his mind.

He wanted Sam back in his bed, preferably tonight.

But he was a patient man. Some things were worth waiting for.

She handed him a plate with a knife and fork. He reached into the basket and unwrapped the fresh smoked sausage and the crusty bread.

Their arms moved within inches of each other. Louis teased her by reaching so close that she drew back a little to avoid contact. The hairs on their arms almost brushed.

But not quite.

The warm air between them crackled with volatile energy created by the absence of contact. He couldn't remember ever hurting so badly for a woman's touch.

A woman who might be his stepmother.

Four

Sam took a bite of the spicy sausage. The boat engine throbbed in a steady pulse, and water slapped against the sides.

She could feel Louis's eyes on her as she licked her lips. His gaze oozed over her like fresh honey. She should be offended that a man she barely knew felt free to stare at her like that.

Except that she'd already slept with him.

"Were all your husbands older than you?"

Louis's strange question jerked her out of a sensual fog. "*All* my husbands." She grimaced. "You make me sound like Zsa Zsa Gabor."

"I think she made them wait until they put a ring on her finger before she slept with them." He winked and bit off a chunk of bread.

Sam's mouth fell open. Then she drew in a breath and reached for her sense of humor. "You're right. Why buy the cow when you can get the milk for free?"

Her mother had repeated that phrase many times during her teen years, when Sam was competing to be Miss Corn Dog or whatever title came with the pageant of that week.

She frowned. "In fact, I was a virgin when I married my first husband." She looked right at Louis. "And yes, he was older."

Louis's expression didn't reveal any opinion, negative or otherwise. "What went wrong?"

"Who knows?" She shrugged and looked out at the waving grasses. The sun hung low on the horizon, bathing land and water in a thick golden soup of light.

"*You* probably do."

She glanced up. People didn't usually talk to her like this. *Like what?*

Rude.

But Louis just watched her, eyes twinkling with mischief as he ate.

"Okay. Let's see. I married him so I could get away from home because my mother ran me on the pageant circles like I was a prize bull and I knew I'd never get to go to college as long as there was a penny to be earned from parading me in front of an audience. To be brutally frank, I'd probably have married anyone."

"I doubt it. Who was he?"

She rankled at his dismissive comment. "He owned a car dealership in our town. He was safe and solid, and he treated me nicely."

"Did you get to go to college?"

Sam's gut tightened. *He's already figured out the answer.* She studied his face for mockery, prepared to defend herself, but all she saw in his eyes was warm interest.

"He didn't want his wife working or going to school."

"Jealous."

"Exactly. And after two years of trying to be the perfect little wife, I'd had enough."

"See? You know exactly why you divorced him." Louis shifted his legs as he cut the engine. The wet cotton of his pants clung to his muscled calves. A reminder of the strength and power of his body. How he'd held her close and…

She averted her gaze. She'd certainly never had feelings like that for her first husband.

Or even her third.

Guilt snaked through her. How could she have fallen so quickly into another man's arms? She'd promised Tarrant that she didn't miss sex. That she didn't need crude lust or grace-less fumbling to be happy.

So why did her skin tingle at the simple nearness of this man?

Sam inhaled deeply and tried to drag her mind back to the conversation. "You're right. I do know why I divorced him. It's amazing I lasted two full years. He barely let me leave the house. I'd been so looking forward to figuring out who I was, without my mother telling me what to wear and say and do, but he was even worse. My every move reflected positively or negatively on the Bob MacClackery Automotive empire. If he could have bought a Barbie doll and dressed it himself and called it Mrs. MacClackery, that would have been heaven for him. Lord knows I tried to please him, but it just wasn't possible. Finally I gave up."

Funny how she could look back with detachment now. Things that had been so painful and hard to cope with at the time now seemed funny. Her desperate attempt to be little Mrs. Perfect, polishing linoleum and hovering over racks of lamb.

And answering to the name of Samantha MacClackery.

"I'm glad your smile is back, but don't forget to eat." Louis spooned more potato salad on her plate.

"How can I eat when you're distracting me with all these bad memories?"

"My humble apologies. Champagne to celebrate your freedom?"

She started to raise her glass, then her hand froze in midair. Samantha's gut clenched as another drop of pure guilt splashed inside her. "I didn't want to be free. I didn't want Tarrant to die."

The smile faded from Louis's eyes. "I'm sorry, that was insensitive. You loved him a lot."

Chest tight, Sam reached into her pocket for a familiar hankie and dabbed at her eyes. "More than I'd ever imagined. And I'd had a lot of practice by then."

He didn't smile at her attempted levity. "It's great that you finally found someone who made you happy. I guess the third time was the charm, or however that cliché goes."

His words sounded insincere, like he was just being polite. Suddenly she needed him to know that her late husband was not just some old man with a yen for young women.

"Tarrant Hardcastle was the kind of man who adds color and style to the history books. He was brimming with ideas and dreams and schemes and glorious visions, right up until the day he died. It was an honor to be in his presence. I still don't know what he saw in me." She fixed him with a steady gaze, defying him to disagree.

Louis met her gaze, his expression serious. "Maybe he saw someone who could love him for himself, not for his money."

She raised an eyebrow. "How would he know?"

"As a man of vision, I bet he could just tell." A dimple appeared as he smiled. "And you are pretty."

Sam felt herself blushing. What for? It's not like she didn't know she was pretty.

That's what got her roped into all those stinking beauty pageants that had her strutting about like a champion heifer when she should have been taking courses at the community college so she could get a real job.

And she knew she was still pretty now, at thirty-one. She should be, what with all the money and effort that went into it. She supported a whole army of personal trainers and massage therapists and colorists and manicurists.

And Tarrant had insisted she only wear couture originals. He called it a quirk of his.

She'd readily humored him. At the time, she'd explained it to herself and others as another example of his visionary approach to life.

Suddenly her perspective was different.

"Maybe he married me because he wanted to dress me up like a Barbie doll, too?"

"I think you enjoy the Barbie thing yourself. I asked you to dress casual and you look like you're ready to hit a runway somewhere."

Sam glanced down at the rather chic linen outfit she'd chosen. "I guess I can't help it. It's an ingrained habit. I'd probably need a twelve-step program to get me into a pair of Levi's at this point."

Louis grinned. "I bet you'd look cute in a pair of Levi's. But if dressing up makes you happy, what's wrong with that? You can't live your life to meet other people's expectations. You have to do what's right for you."

"Sometimes that's hard to figure out. I guess I'm so used to trying to meet other people's expectations that it's natural to me now."

Louis put his plate down on the floor of the boat. He crossed his arms on his knees and leaned forward. She shrank from the intensity in his gaze, from the focused attention of his sharp mind.

"Sounds like you've spent your life looking for a father figure who'd tell you what to do." Again, his gaze wasn't accusatory. If anything, it was compassionate.

She lifted her chin. She didn't want his pity or anyone else's. "As it happens, my father didn't tell me what to do. He mostly ignored me."

Louis scraped his plate into the water. Sam watched in awe as several fish spooked to the surface and snatched at morsels of potato and sausage.

She clung more tightly to her own plate.

Why was she here? She didn't need to be psychoanalyzed by some guy who thought he was God's gift to women. She was just trying to make it through the day in one piece.

Louis cocked his head. "Maybe you were subconsciously trying to get your father's attention by reenacting the scenario."

Sam narrowed her eyes. "I got his attention all right. He hasn't spoken to me since my first divorce. He said I was a sinner for leaving my marriage and doomed to hell." Sam's heart still clenched at the memory. Her plate shook in her hand and she clutched it tighter.

Louis winced. "Some people shouldn't be parents."

He took her plate from her and cleaned it with the same deft move. She watched the fish dart to the surface and inhale her uneaten morsels.

"Recycling in action," he murmured, as he wrapped the plates in a pretty dishcloth and returned them to the basket. "Don't let your dad get you down. I survived just fine without one."

His level gaze challenged her to alter that bare and apparently comfortable fact of his life.

For a second, she felt a twinge of remorse that she'd invaded his comfortable existence and inserted a new possibility into it. "Family can be a wonderful thing."

"In moderation." Louis winked.

Sam smiled. His warm expression disarmed her. The rich copper rays of slow sunset shone on his too-handsome face and glittered in the droplets of water that splattered his powerful forearms.

She tried not to notice the funny ticklish sensation in her belly.

"At least I don't have to worry about making a child miserable by inflicting my own traumas on them."

"Why not?" he asked. "Isn't that part of the fun of parenting?"

Sam felt her smile fade. "I don't have any children." She could say it calmly, all emotion buried beneath a composed exterior. She'd officially given up all hope and she was fine with that. She'd known when she married Tarrant that he was not capable of giving her a child, and she accepted it as her fate.

She'd actually felt calmer since then.

"Me, neither." Louis sipped his wine.

"Do you want children?" It didn't feel forward to ask. They weren't dating. She was just curious.

"Nope."

"Why not?"

"I already told you I'm the product of a chance meeting between a double bass and a saxophone. I grew up like a stream of notes in the air. I don't think I finished an entire year of school in the same place. I certainly never did homework or ate square meals or tried out for a team. I wouldn't have the first clue about raising a child." His eyes sparkled, still squinting slightly against the low rays of sunlight. "So, it's lucky I've never wanted to try."

"You are lucky. It's kind of pathetic how badly I used to want one. And when I married my second husband, who was also keen to have a child, we couldn't get pregnant. We tried day in and day out for months on end."

She reached for her glass and swiped a sip. Ugly memories rolled over her. "He blamed me. We had me tested and everything looked fine, but he wouldn't get tested himself. One day we just stopped having sex. He said he didn't want children anymore."

Louis listened with compassion in his eyes.

"After that, he started staying out a lot. I dressed up in all the lacy lingerie I could find, but he just wasn't interested. 'Working late,' he said, but I soon found out different. And that's when I left him."

Louis whistled. "What a jerk. He didn't know how lucky he was just to have you."

Sam shrugged. "Or not. Apparently I couldn't give him what he wanted." Goose bumps sprang up on her arms and she raised her hands to rub them. "Tarrant appreciated me just for being me. And, oh, boy, was I grateful for that after my first two husbands."

"Finally, you found the father who gave you the love and approval you wanted." Louis looked steadily at her.

Sam recoiled from his suggestion. "No! It wasn't like that at all."

"Did you have sex?"

"Well, no, but... He was ill."

Louis made a small movement with his mouth. Like he

couldn't quite find the right words. Or maybe he could, but he didn't like to say them.

"He was my *husband,* not my father." Her voice rose high as emotion snapped through her.

Louis simply nodded. "And you were a good wife to him. Every man should be so lucky."

Samantha didn't offer any sign of acknowledgment. She didn't need his condescension. She *had* been a good wife.

"I'm not mocking you." Louis frowned. He scratched at something on his arm, pulling his shirt cuff up to reveal a stretch of tanned forearm.

Not that she cared.

He looked up at her. "You're a very giving person. That's a rare and beautiful thing. It's something not everyone appreciates."

Sam found herself wanting to take the compliment and bask in its unfamiliar light. But she managed to resist. "Well, it's been fun analyzing my personal failures and foibles, but let's shine a spotlight on yours for a moment, shall we?"

A wicked grin crept slowly across his mouth. "You're assuming I have any."

He leaned away and started the engine. The movement gave her an extravagant view of the thick muscles of his back under the strained cotton of his shirt.

He wasn't perfect. He probably had all kinds of things wrong with him.

On the other hand, she certainly couldn't find fault with his performance in bed. Of course, her experience in that realm hadn't been of the highest quality.

Until last night.

Okay, so maybe he had the right to be a little cocky.

His honey-toned eyes gazed at her from under thick black lashes that were wasted on a man.

The nerve! He was flirting with her.

She flicked an imaginary crumb off her lap. "I'm sure you're not quite as perfect as you'd like to think you are."

"Probably not, but you'd have to get to know me better to find out." He raised a brow.

"If it turns out that you're my husband's son, then I hope we'll become very close."

"And if it turns out I'm not, you'll cast me aside like a used Ziploc bag?"

A smile tugged at his sensual mouth. Sam blinked.

What if he wasn't Tarrant's son?

Then it was okay to have slept with him. She could even sleep with him again.

A thick sensation swelled inside her and her nipples tingled. She'd never felt *anything* like last night. Every millimeter of her body had come alive with pleasure. A stray throb of memory stirred inside her.

Sam dragged herself back to the present. "I guess we'll cross that bridge when we come to it."

Louis made a show of looking around. The sunset shone like spilled champagne over the wide, shimmering swamp.

"I don't see any bridge. Just a boat, with a man and a woman in it."

Sam glanced around. There really was nothing out there. They'd motored far away from the boathouse and there wasn't a visible structure anywhere. Just sky and bayou, with the sun hovering at the horizon like a cherry floating in a cocktail.

"It's going to get dark any minute."

"Yes."

"Won't we get lost? Or eaten alive by bugs?"

"You're not worried about alligators?" He cocked his head.

Sam shivered. "Thanks for reminding me. Shouldn't we be getting back?"

"We could. Or we could spend the night here." He inclined his head. A wooden structure appeared among the grasses like a mushroom sprouting. A tiny cottage of some sort, on stilts that raised it over the swamp.

"What is it?"

"My granddad's fishing retreat. I renovated it a couple of years ago. It's a lot more high-tech than it looks. I'm embarrassed to say that there's even solar-powered air-conditioning." He shot her a wry smile.

She stiffened. "I'm not sleeping here. You need to take me back to the city."

"Why? It's a beautiful night. You already agreed to spend the evening with me, so I know you don't have anywhere to go. I've proved to you that I can keep my hands off you, and I promise to keep them to myself all night long."

He held up his hands and examined them, as if making sure they were going to behave. "Don't you trust me?"

"I don't have any…stuff with me. Makeup remover. That kind of thing."

"What happens if you don't take your makeup off?" He looked genuinely interested.

Sam hesitated. "I have no idea. I've never tried."

"Then maybe it's time you did. You said you wanted to step outside your comfort zone, didn't you? And really, you can trust me."

Sam rubbed her arm. She felt chilly, though the air was still warm.

"Or maybe it's yourself you don't trust." He squinted

against the sun's rays, looking unbearably handsome. Somehow the fact that he knew it didn't diminish his appeal at all.

"It's peaceful here. No TV, no radio, no Internet. No outside world." The boat had somehow sidled up alongside the building, and he cut the engine.

Water lapped against the wooden stilts holding the structure above the shimmering water. The pinkish cedar looked fresh and new, and she could smell its pungent scent, crisp and inviting amid the fecund funk of the bayou.

The boat rocked in the water. Could it hurt to go inside for just a minute?

"Take a look. See what you think. If you don't like it, we'll head back."

"Okay." She could hardly believe she'd agreed, but suddenly she had to see what Louis DuLac's special place looked like inside.

She could tell it was special. Even from the boat, she could make out images of cranes carved right into the wood of the corner boards and the door, which gave the building a Japanese feel. Steps came down right to the water, each riser carved in a distinct shape, almost like stepping stones.

She hesitated, wondering how to get from the yawing boat onto the solid wood of the steps.

"Since you don't want me to give you a hand up, I'll pull the boat up close to the steps, and you can grab on to the railing."

Louis leaned forward and grabbed the railing himself, then tugged the boat alongside it with the sheer strength of his body. Sam tried not to notice the way his muscles rippled under his shirt and how his powerful thighs braced to hold the boat steady. "Go ahead."

Sam climbed shakily to her feet. She leaned out of the boat

to grab the railing. True to his promise, Louis held the boat steady against the steps while she pulled herself up onto them.

Apprehension prickled along her spine as she stood there on the steps of the only structure visible for miles around. If he turned the boat around and left, she'd be stranded.

But he lashed the boat to a stilt with expert ease. "Go on in, it's unlocked."

"You just leave it open?"

He shrugged. "If someone's determined enough, they'll get in anyway."

Sam pushed open the smooth door, with its lovely square carving of two cranes amid tall grasses.

"Oh, goodness." It was beautiful. Dark golden light filled the space, streaming through a wide window on the opposite side that framed the sunset. Considering the warmth of the afternoon, the interior was wonderfully cool and comfortable.

The plank floor invited her feet to step inside. The single room smelled of fresh, new wood. The scent of new beginnings.

Louis came in behind her and hesitated. She shifted aside, giving him room to pass without touching her. Her skin tingled as he eased into the space, sliding by her *almost* close enough to touch, but not quite. His male scent mingled with the fresh aroma of cedar to push her senses into overdrive.

She watched as he flipped a latch on the paneled wall and pulled down something like a Murphy bed. It opened to a low sofa, Japanese style, with a patterned covering of dark purple and gray. He pulled a couple of cushions out of the cavity in the wall where the sofa had been. "Take a load off."

Sam eased herself down onto the sofa. Its cushiony soft surface felt blissful after the hard bench of the boat. Louis moved across the room and pulled down an identical sofa on the other side. "See? No touching required. His and hers."

"This place is amazing. What else is hidden in these walls?"

Louis beamed with what looked like pride as he pulled open another paneled cabinet to reveal the interior of a fridge, stocked with drinks. "What can I get you?"

"Oh, my." Sam stretched out on the cushioned surface. Her muscles crackled as tension slipped from them. "This does feel good. Maybe a soda water."

The delicious whoosh of the soda bottle cap popping off made her mouth water. She took the bottle and again their fingers almost touched, but not quite. She could swear she'd felt a snap of electrical current right at the tip of her fingers.

She smiled. He smiled back. A warm sensation stirred in her belly.

Uh-oh.

Get a grip, Sam. You're probably the fourth woman he's brought here this week. "This is quite the romantic hideaway. I'm guessing it gets a lot of use," she said drily. She took a sip of her soda water. The bubbles crackled over her tongue.

"I come here a lot." He looked steadily at her. "More all the time."

A prick of jealousy stuck her somewhere uncomfortable.

"But you're the first woman I've ever brought here."

"What?" A weird shiver sprang across her skin.

"This is where I come to be alone. Don't get me wrong, I like people. I love the hustle and bustle of my restaurants and organizing events and bringing people together. That's been my whole life."

He pushed a hand through his hair and turned to look out the window. The sun was now a slim chip of glowing amber, resting delicately above the dark purple horizon. "Maybe I'm getting older or something." He looked at her, humor shining in his eyes. "Who am I kidding? Of course I'm getting older.

But lately, I find I need to step off the carousel and reconnect with nature. With myself."

He frowned, as if embarrassed by his confession. "And I thought you might like to do that, too."

A very strange sensation rose inside Sam. She absolutely believed him. He'd chosen her, out of all the women in the world—a good percentage of whom would no doubt be willingly at his disposal—to share his special place with.

Without the promise of even a touch, let alone a kiss.

That touched her somewhere far more powerful and vulnerable than her skin.

She covered her confusion with a sip of her drink. She wondered if she should say something, but Louis didn't seem to expect her to. He'd brought in the picnic basket and he opened it and unloaded some supplies into the small fridge. "We have fruit and cheese if you're hungry, and there's plenty of bread left. If you like, we could catch some shrimp. There's a grill out on the deck."

Sam laughed. "That's self-sufficient! Let's leave the shrimp alone, though. They deserve some peace and quiet, too. How did you come to build way out here?"

"My granddad owned the land." Louis popped the cap off a second bottle of soda water. She watched his powerful neck swell as he took a swig. "Or at least it used to be land." He smiled ruefully. "It's been underwater for as long as I can remember, but he said it used to be dry and that you could walk out here from the road."

"That's hard to imagine."

"I like it better like this. Somehow a destination seems more worthwhile if there's a bit of a journey to get there."

"I guess you'd have to have that perspective if you have restaurants all over the world and travel a lot."

"I grew up traveling. My mom's a singer, so I went with her on tour every summer."

"That must have been fun."

"Fun, exhausting, confusing, exciting. A little bit of everything. Made me who I am, though. I make friends easily and I can settle in pretty much anywhere at a moment's notice. One of my friends teases me that the whole reason I opened my restaurants is so I can have a roomful of friends to drop in on in any city I visit."

"That's a nice idea."

Louis chuckled. "I think she might just be right."

Sam's smile faltered at the mention of a "she." Which was ridiculous. How on earth could she be jealous of some woman she'd never even heard of who probably really was only a friend?

Especially when she had no real personal relationship with him *at all*.

Other than being the first woman invited to his special place.

And having spent one night in his bed.

The memory of his strong arms around her assaulted her like an anxiety attack. He'd rolled up his sleeves and she could see his powerful forearms clearly, even in the dusky gloom. The exertion of their journey had rendered him rather rumpled. His hair curled untidily over his forehead and his pants had dried into wrinkles. He looked more boyish and innocent than he had yesterday, as the elegant and worldly host of his own smart restaurant.

She probably looked pretty rumpled, too, though she managed to resist peeking down at her clothes to check. Lord knew what this humidity was doing to her hair.

Then again, maybe she also looked cute and girlish.

She tried not to giggle. Suddenly she felt like a teenager.

For the first time in her life, she was alone, in a sexually charged situation—let's face it, the sexual tension was so thick in the air she could smell it even over all the cedar—with a man her own age.

"I bet you're a painter." Louis's low voice jarred her out of her contemplation.

"You mean, painting pictures?"

He nodded. "When you look at things you seem to linger and take in all the elements of the image in front of your eyes."

Sam blinked. Her heart started pounding. "I, uh, used to paint...a little."

"What did you paint?"

"Landscapes, flowers, that kind of thing. Nothing at all serious or important."

"In whose opinion? One of your not-so-nice ex-husbands?"

She swallowed. "Well, yes. Tarrant always said I should paint, though. He offered to set up a studio for me in our house."

"But?" He cocked his head.

"I was too busy." She shrugged. "Being his wife was a full-time job."

"All the ladies' lunches, the pedicure appointments, the charity fund-raising meetings, the gala evenings." His voice trailed off.

Sam flushed. He'd reduced her whole busy life to a dismissive sentence. She lifted her chin. "Exactly."

"Now that you're alone, you could make the time."

"Maybe I don't want to." She fiddled with her ring.

"Afraid to see what might pop out of your imagination with no one to tell you what to do?"

"I'm not sure I even have an imagination anymore."

"Of course you do." Louis narrowed his eyes. "It's just

been lying dormant, letting ideas and fantasies and dreams stockpile in there, waiting for the moment you choose to set them free."

Sam frowned. Her mind felt as blank and lusterless as an unprimed canvas. Something she never could have imagined when she was a teenager with a million dreams. "I don't think so."

Undeterred, Louis leaned forward, a gleam in his eyes. "If you could paint something right now, anything, what would it be?"

The warm glow of the last rays of sunset picked out the smooth, strong planes of his face, molding them like a fine statue. How magnificent he'd look standing there, nude, with those coppery rays chiseling the sturdy musculature of his body.

Uh-oh. Her imagination appeared to be working after all.

"Come on. Anything."

"The sunset, maybe," she said, hesitant, afraid to meet the pull of his gaze.

"Then let's go look at it." He rose to his feet and stepped toward her, then stopped, as if he'd just remembered that invisible glass wall between them. Sam's skin tingled once again at the absence of natural contact.

He pushed open a door in the wall, and the room flooded with light like thick golden honey. "There's a deck out here. Come on."

Squinting against the sudden brightness, Sam followed him outside. The entire bayou was aflame with gold and copper. Rich dark reds and purples hung in the trees, the water shimmered and glimmered as its black depths reflected the last rays of sun with diamond brightness.

"I challenge you to find anything more beautiful than that

in the whole world." Louis gazed out at the jeweled world before them.

"It's magical."

He turned to her, and a laugh escaped. "It is magic, and it's going to work its magic on you. The old voodoo everyone talks about. It's going to flood your imagination with beauty until it overflows and you just can't keep it locked up anymore."

Sam tried to suppress a giggle, but it came out anyway. She imagined attacking her dull life with a brush loaded with bright golden-yellow paint.

Not that she'd know where to begin.

"I couldn't paint this. I don't have the skills. I always wanted to take a class, but somehow it just never happened."

"So start tomorrow."

"I can't."

"Why not?"

"For one thing, I'm too old."

Louis snorted. "Unless you've had some really fine plastic surgery, I wouldn't put you a day over thirty."

A flash of vain pride swelled inside her, and she cursed herself for it. "I'm thirty-one."

"See? You're practically a kid."

"I'm not. I'm a widow with a large charitable trust to manage. It's an important responsibility."

"And I admire you for taking it on, but trust me, there is absolutely enough time, both in your day and in the rest of your life, for you to become the painter you always wanted to be."

"What if I stink at it?"

"That kind of thinking keeps people glued to their TVs watching other people live while they wonder what real living would be like. You're not going to do that. You've got a decade or two of living to catch up on, from the sound of things."

Sam looked out at the bright palette of colors shimmering around her. Suddenly the world felt rich and heavy with possibilities.

Louis leaned over the railing. "I've got a friend in New York, Margo, who teaches at Pratt Institute. I'll give her a call and she'll help you get started."

Excitement crackled through Sam. Could it really be that easy? To just pick up a brush and get started? "I might need a good supply of nude male models."

Louis grinned. "I can see your imagination's up and running."

"Once again, I can see you have an unsettling amount of insight into me."

He shrugged. "Someone's got to set you free."

"I am free. I make my own decisions."

"Do you? Or are you going to unwittingly start looking for another father figure to tell you what to do?"

Irritation prickled over her. "Seriously, Tarrant was not a father figure."

"I'm just calling it the way I see it." He opened the door to the cabin. "We'd better go back in before the bugs start biting."

Sam followed him into the dimly lit space.

Although she hated to admit it, her previous partners had all been at least ten years older.

She'd always felt older than her peers. With her strict and easily angered parents, she hadn't had the opportunity to be a moody teenager. One time, she'd broken a vase while dancing around the room to the radio, and she'd eaten only cold cereal with water for a week as a punishment.

Her mother had pointed out that in addition to making her more careful in the future, it would slim her down for the upcoming teen pageant she was entered in.

She'd learned to toe every line like an infantry recruit out of sheer self-preservation. She'd never even attempted to do anything wild and irresponsible.

Like sleeping with a man she'd just met.

Sam knew Tarrant had wed her because she'd refused to sleep with him until they were married.

He'd said that was so audacious that he fell instantly in love with her. They were married a week later.

Louis was the only man she'd ever slept with that she wasn't married to.

The final fiery rays of the setting sun licked around him, setting her imagination aflame with how sensational he'd look and feel if he were naked in her arms. Right now.

God help her, she wanted to sleep with him again.

"I need to go back. *Now.*"

Five

"No problem." Louis moved back inside and closed up his sofa.

Sam stared at him. He was just going to agree and take her back without a fight? Her heart sank a little.

She followed him in. It was almost dark and she felt disoriented. Louis closed her bed and ushered her to the door.

Didn't he want her to stay?

Goose bumps rose on her skin at the thought of leaving the comfortable cedar-scented haven for the dark and murky swamp.

He held the door open. Their arms almost brushed as she passed him and the tiny hairs on her skin stood up as if trying to reach out and touch him.

He latched the door, eased by her on the steps—so close she could feel the heat from his skin—and jumped lightly down into the boat moored off to one side. "Stay there, I'll bring it right under the steps for you."

Sam hesitated. Surely if she stepped down, the boat could rock and she'd lose her footing? Night creatures chattered and chirped in the bayou all around. Louis crouched in the boat, looking at her, his expression unreadable in the deep dusk.

It would all be so easy if she could just take his hand to steady herself while she stepped down.

But she'd made the rules so she had to stick to them. She sucked in a shaky breath. One, two, three, she launched herself forward and managed to land one foot on the wooden floor of the skiff. The other foot, however, caught on the rim of the boat and she lost her balance and stumbled forward.

"Whoa!" Louis caught her in his arms before she could plummet to the hard wood.

Her body collided with his in what felt like slow motion. First, her hands crashed into his chest, then somehow slid under his armpits to grab around his waist.

Louis almost lost his balance, too, as she fell into him on the uneven surface.

Her breasts crushed against hard muscle before she finally came to rest, sprawled over him like a car wrapped around a lamppost.

"Whoops," she murmured. A hot shiver of desire flashed through her at the feel of his hard muscle under her.

Her pelvis rested awkwardly on his. A sudden thickening beneath his zipper aroused feverish memories that made her insides start to throb.

Sam sprang back, her face heating. "I'm so sorry."

"I'm not," he croaked. "I'm just sorry you're on this no-touching kick. Unless this is your way of telling me you didn't really mean it?"

Even in the semi-darkness, she saw a wicked gleam in his eye.

Heat crept through her like fire along a fuse. Her breasts felt heavy, and her skin stung with awareness.

She scrambled backward, her hands pressed to his hard chest and belly as she peeled herself off his strong body with painful regret.

"I meant it."

I wish I didn't, but I did.

"Just think, I might take this DNA test and you'll find out I'm not related to your husband."

Sam blinked. "It's a possibility."

A very attractive one.

He cocked his head. "Then things would be different." His smooth voice caressed her in the near darkness.

"Very different. But for now, let's just get back, okay?"

"Okay."

In less than five minutes, she was clambering out of the boat onto dry land and back into his vintage car. Her legs felt hollow and her chest strangely empty.

Even if he wasn't Tarrant's son, she'd still only been widowed six months. It was far too soon for any kind of…affair.

And hadn't she promised herself she was done with all that stuff? Three husbands were enough for one lifetime. She planned to devote herself to managing Tarrant's charities.

And get a nice cat.

"Buckle in." He slid in beside her. Painful awareness of his body only inches from hers made her fight not to squirm in her seat. He was so healthy and strong and young and…sexy.

Different from Tarrant.

Guilt tightened her gut again. Her love for Tarrant had been based on so much more than mere physical attraction. He was a handsome man, of course, but older and unwell. The appeal was more cerebral. Spiritual, even. She'd wanted to help him.

To save him.

And in a small way she had, at least for a time.

Finding his two long-lost sons had awakened something in him that made him better able to handle his own mortality. He had a sense of the future, a conviction that he'd left behind a legacy more powerful than bricks and mortar and money in the bank.

And Louis could well be a part of that legacy.

"You will take the DNA test, won't you?"

"Of course. I promised I'd take it if you had dinner with me. You held up your part of the bargain, so I wouldn't be a gentleman if I didn't hold up mine." He turned to her and she could see his appealing grin in the light reflected from the headlights.

The sun had disappeared, leaving them shrouded in darkness. A cool breeze whipped her hair as they drove along the winding, lonely road through the bayou country.

"Thank you. I appreciate it." Although it was obvious he wasn't a man used to taking orders, he'd literally obeyed every single one of her stipulations.

An odd feeling snuck through her. She wasn't used to that kind of respect from a man. Much as she'd cared for Tarrant, he made all the rules and everyone else fell into line. A pattern she was familiar—even somewhat comfortable with—from her first two marriages.

But Louis let her call the shots. He didn't feel the need to bully her or exert his manly dominance. Yet he exuded natural self-possession. Effortless confidence.

Which of course was how he had managed to get her out in a boat on a swamp in the dark.

"Why are you laughing?" His rich voice trickled into her ear.

"I'm just trying to figure out how you talked me into this."

"I didn't talk you into anything. You wanted to come. You just weren't aware of it at the time."

"Oh. Is that it?" She chuckled. "I guess you can tell all this because you inherited your grandmother's psychic abilities. What do I want to do next?"

"Well, you want to come back to my home and spend the night in bed, then wake up early and eat beignets and milky coffee on the riverbank with me, but you're not going to."

"I don't even know what a *beignet* is."

"And you're not going to find out, either, since you have no intention of staying over at my house. Which is a shame, because we'll both miss out on another wonderful night together."

The way he said it, soft and wistful, tugged at something deep inside her. "It was a nice night. And so was this. But you do understand, don't you?"

"I respect your wishes." He flashed a glance at her. "And I have a feeling you're not used to that, so I'm hoping it helps my case." A wicked smile flashed across his mouth.

"Your insight into me is a little frightening, truth be told."

He looked out into the distance. "Don't let it worry you. I can see into everyone." He turned to look at her again, and even in the dark she could see the honeyed shimmer of his eyes. "And in you, I like what I see."

Sam rubbed her arms as a strange hot-cold feeling cascaded over her.

Why did it feel so good that this almost-stranger liked her? That he cared enough to chase her, and then to respect her wishes?

Maybe she was just relieved that someone could spend the night with her and still want more.

She fiddled with her ring, not sure how he'd react to her next request. "I'd like to come with you to the lab. Then we can arrange to have the results sent to both of us, if you agree."

"Don't trust me to tell you my secrets?" He smiled, looking out the windshield. "And there I flattered myself thinking you might be starting to trust me."

"I am."

And that's why I need to know the truth.

Shivers of excitement rippled through her at the possibility that he could be no relation at all. That maybe they could…

She fanned her face, suddenly hot. She was getting way ahead of herself.

What if he was Tarrant's son?

How on earth would she explain to Tarrant's daughter, Fiona, that she'd slept with her half brother?

Her insides clenched into a knot at the thought.

Fiona had hated Sam for marrying Tarrant despite being young enough to be his daughter herself. They'd eventually formed an uneasy truce, which had lately warmed into a careful friendship as a result of Sam's persistent efforts.

A revelation like this could be catastrophic.

She wouldn't tell her. She couldn't. Keeping Tarrant's family together was the *most* important thing in her life.

Without them she had no one.

"You can come with me. I won't even put any conditions on it." He glanced at her, and she tried to ignore the heat that flared inside her, despite her fears. "And you can have them send you the results directly. I don't have any secrets."

Sam's stomach tightened. "Will you keep our…encounter a secret? Just for now, until we know?"

Louis frowned at her. "I don't go around bragging about

my personal business. But it doesn't sit right with me to be secretive. We don't have anything to be ashamed of."

The "we" gave her a strange thrill, followed by a rush of shame. Was she so lonely and desperate that she craved even such an unsuitable encounter?

"It's just that…Tarrant's daughter. She wouldn't understand."

"She wouldn't understand that two consenting adults can enjoy each other's company?"

"Not if we're related."

Louis laughed. "It's not like you're my first cousin, sweetheart. I know you New Yorkers hear all kind of stories about us down here in the deep South, but you and I aren't related by blood."

"You know what I mean. It's taken me a long time to get close to her. Please." She hated the pleading tone in her voice.

Louis stared out over the wheel. The headlights created twin yellow flares on the road surface. The hum and flutter of nature was almost deafening in the darkness around them. "I won't say anything."

His gruff tone underlined his reluctance. Sam felt a momentary stab of guilt at making him undermine his principles, but really, who would he tell anyway?

They passed the rest of the drive chatting about music and movies. Careful conversation. Witty, but guarded, like two acquaintances at a party.

Which was what they were. She didn't know him, and he didn't know her. Not after one night. Or even two.

He parked near her hotel. Nervous energy fluttered through her. He opened her door and stood aside with mock deference to her insistence on no touching.

Her body ached at the lack of even conventional contact.

"Good night," she said, her voice shaking. She glanced at the brightly lit entrance of the hotel. They stood in the muted glow of a vintage streetlamp.

"It was a good night. And I think a good-night peck on the cheek would only be polite."

Sam hesitated. Swallowed. Her rules were a bit silly, rude even. And he'd been so understanding and wonderful about it. Surely just a little, tiny, goodbye type of kiss wouldn't be so bad?

Anxiety and excitement snaked through her. He stepped toward her and she instinctively tilted her chin.

An electric sensation zapped through her as her cheek brushed his. *Uh-oh.* Before she could stop, her lips found his.

Hot relief rushed through her when their mouths met and mingled. Her arms found their way around his waist and her fingers buried themselves in his cotton shirt, gripping the sturdy muscle underneath.

Louis's arms closed around her back, soft and reassuring. He kissed her tenderly, with restraint, even as passion snapped and sizzled in the air around them.

Oh, dear.

When they finally parted, disentangling their limbs with agonizing reluctance, her whole body throbbed and tingled with painful arousal.

"I'm not sure that was such a great idea," she rasped.

Louis didn't say anything. He just looked at her, his expression…pained. His arousal was visible even in the dim glow from the streetlight.

She could tell he was thinking, *If it wasn't for your neurotic reluctance, we'd spend the night in each other's arms the way you know we both want to.*

But she couldn't.

"Um. The test. What time is good tomorrow?"

Louis raised an eyebrow, then blew out a hard breath. "Let's get it over with. The earlier the better."

"The lab opens at nine."

"I'll pick you up here."

"Great." She managed a fake smile and practically ran for the bright sanctuary of the hotel lobby. She didn't dare look back. She knew he was standing there, looking after her.

Waiting for her to weaken and run back into his arms.

Her hands trembled as she pulled her key card from her pocket. She stepped into the glittering, polished interior of the elevator and the doors closed, leaving her alone.

Phew. She'd done it. He'd agreed to take the test and she'd managed the entire evening without any inappropriate contact.

Except that kiss.

But really, it was just a kiss. Practically a peck on the cheek.

A sound escaped her mouth. A snort of disbelief. Her whole body still stung with stray energy that snuck over her skin and along her nerves, from her lips to her fingers and toes and everywhere in between.

She stepped out into the silent, carpeted hallway and shivered in the air-conditioning. She fumbled with the key in the lock, but managed to open the door and step into her luxurious suite with its magnificent scrolled bed and five-hundred-count sheets.

Alone.

Oh, Tarrant. Why did you have to die and leave me?

The familiar lament rang through her mind. It hurt so much to go to bed by herself every night, the cold sheets a reminder that she had no one to comfort her. No one to hold her. No one to mutter and sigh over the day's mundane events or admire the silly new lingerie she'd bought just to make him smile.

Louis might do all those things, if she'd let him.

But for how long? A week? A month?

Then he'd be off to Paris or Milan and the busy whirl of his life. Back to all the other women he no doubt charmed and delighted just like her.

She and Louis were the same age and while she'd been married three times, he'd never taken the plunge once. *That should tell you something.*

Even if he wasn't potentially her stepson, there was no possibility of a lasting relationship.

He was exactly what she didn't need. Another opportunity for the papers to fill their pages with humiliating gossip and innuendo.

He was *all wrong*.

But that didn't stop her from clutching the sheets around her and wishing with every ounce of hope she had left that he wasn't Tarrant's son after all.

Morning sunlight sparkled off the sidewalks and windows as Sam and Louis walked the few blocks from the hotel to the lab. She was glad of the excuse to wear large, dark glasses that hid her emotions.

She noticed with a start that they paused to wait for a car to pass at exactly the same spot where she'd seen the sign for *Madame Ayida ~ Palmistry and spiritual consultations.*

The black letters danced in front of her eyes.

"I went to that fortune-teller yesterday." She pointed to the sign. "Madame Ayida. What she told me made me decide to have dinner with you so you'd agree to the test."

"I owe Madame Ayida a debt of gratitude."

"She told me to follow my heart." Sam frowned as she remembered the gravity in the young woman's voice.

"That's good advice. Did your heart tell you to keep your hands off me, or did it tell you to kiss me?"

Both.

Sam brushed away his question with a laugh. "She also said I had to choose between two roads, one familiar and one strange, and that the choice would determine the rest of my life."

Louis looked at her. Sunlight glittered in his honey-gold eyes and the force of his gaze made her belly quiver.

She bit her lip. "Do you think fate is determined in advance by forces we can't control or do you think we create our own destiny?"

"Definitely the latter. Every decision you make shapes your life."

"Sometimes I feel like I'm on a roller coaster and the best I can do is hang on. Every plan I make gets derailed." She sighed. "I used to think I just made the wrong choices in the first place, but since Tarrant died, I don't feel in control at all. I feel I could have saved him, somehow. That I should have."

He frowned. "I guess you're right that we have no control over some things. I don't have any control over who my father is."

"Or isn't."

Louis had a strange expression in his eyes. "I have a funny feeling the tests are going to tell you what you want to hear."

Sam froze. He assumed that she wanted to find out he was the missing heir she sought.

But he was wrong.

"You never know. You don't look all that much like him."

"I take after my mother."

"You do. I've seen her album covers. She's very beautiful." The dark, exotic beauty fit the mold of so many of Tarrant's former lovers. Sam felt a bit pale and colorless by comparison.

Or maybe just jealous.

Tarrant had played Bijou DuLac's albums quite often, and they'd even gone to see her in concert at Carnegie Hall once—before Sam knew she was likely the mother of one of his children.

A joy Sam would never personally experience.

The familiar hollow emptiness inside her opened up like a sudden chasm. Sam kept her eyes dead ahead, hoping Louis wouldn't look at her until she got her emotions under control.

"My mom would throw an opera-diva-style tantrum if she knew I was about to take this test."

"She wouldn't want you to know who your father is?"

"She'd see it as irrelevant. She can't stand looking at the past, or even toward the future. She's big on living in the present. Enjoy each day as you meet it head-on, all the ones behind you are irrelevant, and the ones ahead are an adventure you'll greet when you come to it."

"I get the sense you share her philosophy."

"I do. And I've had a pretty damn good life so far, so it's working for me."

Sam's skin prickled as they walked past Madame Ayida's storefront. "How do you feel about finding out who your father is?"

"I guess it's an adventure I'll greet when I come to it." He flashed her a mischievous grin.

They both grew quiet when they reached the door of the lab. A smiling redheaded nurse bustled out to the reception desk to greet them. Sam explained that they needed to collect Louis's DNA and have the results sent to both of them. She didn't bother to explain they'd then be compared to Tarrant's data at the company labs in New York.

She nodded sympathetically. "Of course." She looked at

Louis. "And if the results prove you're the father, you be sure to make your payments on time, unlike my louse of an ex-husband." She turned to wink at Sam.

Sam cringed. "Oh, it's not like that at all."

The redhead shuffled through some papers. "You think he's the father of your child, right? That's why you need the results, too."

"No. We think he's my husband's son."

The nurse glanced up, and squinted at Louis. Then back at Sam, who felt heat rising to her face.

Louis looked totally unruffled. If anything, she saw a gleam of humor in his eye.

Why did she feel the need to explain? "It's complicated."

"I'll bet."

Sam waited in the lobby while Louis went into the back to have his cheek swabbed for cells. The nurse's unprofessional behavior left her rattled. Why did people have to butt into someone else's personal business?

She could just imagine the newspaper headlines if this little story got out.

Louis emerged with a guarded expression on his face, and they didn't talk at all until they were back out on the street.

"I have to go catch a plane," she said quietly to forestall any suggestions he might tempt her with.

Or maybe she was flattering herself that he'd try.

"I'm flying to Paris myself. Big party at my restaurant there tonight. A lot of my oldest friends will be there."

Sam tried to ignore a twinge of jealousy. "Sounds like fun. I hope you have a wonderful time."

He looked at her, golden eyes shining with wary appreciation. "Thank you. I'll call you and we can talk when the results come in."

"Sounds good."

There was no suggestion of even the faintest peck on the cheek. No doubt Louis was also aware that any contact between them might explode into a conflagration neither of them could handle right now.

Sam managed a cheery wave that later seemed forced and phony, but it was the best she could do. Then she hurried away down the sidewalk, heart pounding, wondering if she'd ever see Louis again.

Six

Sam knew the results were due today, so she deliberately lingered in bed, away from the prying eyes of the household. Still, she gulped when her phone rang. Her hand shook as she reached for it and flipped it open.

"Sam, guess what?" Bella's cheery voice sent her pulse into overdrive. Bella ran the Hardcastle lab and was personally overseeing the DNA-test analysis.

"What?" she croaked.

"It's a match! Isn't that great? You found another of Tarrant's sons."

"Oh, fantastic." Her voice seemed to echo in a hollow cavern. "Are you sure?"

She'd almost convinced herself Louis wasn't related. That he was just another one of the billions of people walking the face of the earth who had no relationship with Tarrant Hardcastle.

That he could be simply…hers.

"The results are incontrovertible. Nearly a hundred percent. Which is hardly surprising considering that Louis DuLac is a successful restaurant entrepreneur. Isn't it funny that all three of Tarrant's sons are movers and shakers in the same field? Dominic in food retail, Amado in the wine business and now Louis with an international chain of restaurants. I guess it proves the apple doesn't fall far from the tree, even if the tree wasn't actively involved in its development."

"Yeah. Strange." Sam swallowed. Her heart bumped painfully against her ribs. "Well, that is great news." She tried to inject enthusiasm into her voice, which only made it waver.

It was over. All over.

Well, the self-indulgent stage of their relationship was. No more flirtatious glances or kisses or passionate embraces. The next stage, where she was his cheerful but sexless stepmother—that was just beginning.

She slid a little deeper under the covers. "I'll call and tell him myself."

"May I speak to Louis DuLac, please?"

Pleasure flooded Louis's body at the sound of Sam's voice. Her formal tones brought a smile to his lips.

"Speaking." He sat in his restaurant, going over some orders before the early-lunchtime crowd started to arrive. The ceiling fan wafted air over his skin, which heated at the memory of Sam's sparkling blue eyes and lithe body.

"Great. It's Samantha." Again the clipped voice. As if they were business acquaintances. Like he'd never held her in his arms and made love to her all night long.

"I know. Hi, Sam." He let a hint of flirtation slide into his voice.

"You're Tarrant's son. I just heard the results of the analysis. There's no doubt at all, you're definitely his." The barrage of words ended abruptly.

No words came to his tongue. *Tarrant's son.*

He had a father.

He blew out a snort. Of course he had a father; everyone did. Hard to be born without one. Still. A real person, who probably shared traits with him that he'd never even noticed in himself.

"Are you there?" Sam's voice jerked him out of the strange rush of thoughts.

"Sure, I'm here. It's taking a while to sink in."

"Isn't it wonderful?" Her voice rang with false cheer.

"Yeah, I guess so." She'd wanted so badly for him to be the son she sought. Or did she? Now that they'd been intimate, everything was complicated.

"I'm thrilled." Her voice reached such a high note that it actually cracked. "It's just what I was hoping for. You must come to New York as soon as possible. Your brother Dominic is anxious to meet you, and so is your sister, Fiona. Amado told me he can fly up from Argentina anytime."

"I have two brothers and a sister?" He couldn't keep the excitement out of his voice. She'd mentioned Tarrant's other children before, but they hadn't seemed real until now. A thick rush of emotion flooded his body and made his skin prickle.

Since the loss of his grandparents, he's felt painfully alone sometimes. His mom was…well, she was a law unto herself, and woe betide anyone who tried to count on her for anything other than a spectacular stage performance. His grandma and granddad had been the people he'd turned to for love and support, until suddenly they were gone—dead within weeks of each other.

Adrenaline and excitement pulsed inside him at the prospect of meeting the siblings he never knew he had. "I can't wait to meet them. Truly. Where do I show up? Just tell me when. I'm coming."

"Oh, Louis. I'm so happy. Really, I am." He heard tears in her voice. "Tarrant would be so pleased. It's such a shame you'll never meet him."

"I have a feeling I'll get to know him anyway."

I've already slept with his wife. Regret, mingled with stray longing, stuck in his craw.

There was a pause. "Um, I hate to ask this, but, ah…"

"Will I keep my hands off you?"

"Exactly." The relief in her voice pricked his balloon of enthusiasm a little.

Gain two brothers and a sister…lose a lover.

Not that Samantha had ever been his to lose in any real sense. *His stepmother.* "I'll be the very soul of discretion."

"Sam relax. Why are you so jumpy?" Dominic looked up from the large desk where he was signing some kind of contract. "It's fantastic that you found another one of our brothers."

Sam gulped and glanced around Dominic's spacious office at Hardcastle Enterprises. What on earth would he say if he knew she'd also *slept* with Louis? Tarrant's first son was highly principled, to the point where he'd at first rejected his father out of hand, disgusted by the man who'd abandoned his mother and neglected his responsibilities.

"What time's he coming?" Amado had flown up from Argentina to meet his new brother, and was clearly excited.

"He'll be here any minute," she said, trying to keep the tremor out of her voice.

Dominic surprised her by crossing the room to take her in his arms for a hug. Though standoffish and reluctant to join either the family or the corporation at first, to her great pride and happiness, he'd become their enthusiastic leader. "Sam, you do realize that none of us would be here without you. You're a miracle."

She laughed off his compliment. "Don't be silly. It was all Tarrant's idea."

"You can say that all you like. We know better."

"You're the mother of all of us, Sam," said Amado, while crunching a crudité. "Whether you like it or not." His mischievous grin revealed how happy he was to be here, though at first, he'd refused to even meet his famous father.

Sam blanched. Of course he had no idea how deep his well-meant comment cut her. "Oh, don't be silly." She waved her hand in the air. "I'm more like your sister."

Not that being Louis's sister even by marriage made sleeping with him any more excusable.

"In age, yes, but in wisdom and caring? No. You're our mom." Amado wrapped his arm affectionately around her shoulders and squeezed.

Warmth flooded Sam and made tears well in her eyes. Honestly, she did feel maternal affection for these strong and capable young men.

So how had things gone so horribly wrong with Louis?

Her feelings for him were anything but maternal.

Sam almost jumped out of her skin as the door to Dominic's office opened. Fiona, Tarrant's daughter from his second marriage, marched in. "Louis DuLac has arrived in reception. He's on his way up."

"Oh, goodness." Sam's hand flew to her chest. "That's great. Wonderful." She smiled at Fiona, but the pretty redhead was fiddling with the buttons on her new lavender iPod device. Probably pretending she didn't care one way or another that yet another sibling had shown up to displace her from her former position as Tarrant's only child.

Sam felt for her. She'd managed to become close to the prickly young woman, and didn't want anything to damage their delicate relationship. Yet another reason her accidental liaison with Louis had to remain secret.

She glanced around the bright, comfortable office. Dominic and Amado stood, expectant grins on their faces.

Their wives, Bella and Susannah, were at this very moment helping Fiona hastily arrange the details for a celebration party tonight.

How would Sam react when she saw Louis? His face had haunted her in dreams. Worse yet, so had the touch of his hands and the press of his hard body against hers.

Would she be able to keep her emotions and physical reactions under control when he arrived, or would the bright flush of her face or a sudden tightening of her nipples give her away?

She checked the buttons of her thick Chanel suit. At least no one would see the nipples.

The door flung open again and Sam tried not to topple off her heels. Melissa, Dominic's admin, peered around it. "He's here!" Her smile radiated the joy everyone in the company seemed to feel about the exciting news that Sam had found a new family member.

She should be happiest of all, since it was her avowed mission in life to gather Tarrant's scattered children.

So why did she feel dread trickling through her veins?

Louis appeared in the doorway and his eyes locked instantly onto hers.

"Welcome!" she stammered. "Louis, this is your brother Dominic."

Dominic strode forward and shook his hand, then broke the

tension by pulling Louis into a hug. "We're so glad Sam found you."

"Yeah, me, too." Louis glanced up at Sam with those familiar honey-gold eyes.

Anxiety pooled in her belly, along with the unwelcome thickening of arousal. "And this is your brother Amado. He flew overnight from Argentina to be here when you arrived."

Amado clasped Louis's hand in both of his and shook it forcefully. "I know you probably feel strange right now meeting a crowd of relatives you didn't know you had." His English was accented, but flawless. "Trust me, you get used to it."

"To be honest, it doesn't feel strange at all." Louis looked from Amado to Dominic. "Sam was so convinced I'd be Tarrant's son, that when the DNA test results came back, I wasn't the least bit surprised."

Sam swallowed hard. "Goodness, look at the three of you together." Tarrant's three sons were all so tall and handsome. With their dark hair and olive complexions, they actually looked more like each other than any of them resembled Tarrant. But there was no denying they all had the air of commanding authority that had struck her so strongly when she first met her husband.

Emotion swelled in her chest. "What a wonderful sight. If only Tarrant was here to enjoy it."

Dominic stepped toward her and wrapped his big arm around her shoulders. Probably because he knew too well that memories of Tarrant easily reduced her to a blubbering wreck.

She grabbed his strong hand, sucked in a breath and tried to pull herself together.

I can do this. Her role here was to honor Tarrant's memory as she gathered his family together. She could forget about Louis as a man, and think of him purely as her...son.

Couldn't she?

She sought his face, hoping to reassure herself. But when his eyes locked onto hers, energy flashed between them with defibrillator intensity.

Uh-oh.

"This is the lab." Bella, the head of technical research at Hardcastle Enterprises, beckoned Louis and the others into the bright space, with its gleaming instruments and rows of computers. He'd been in the building for less than an hour, but already Louis thought it was the most outrageous place he'd ever seen.

"When I first showed up, Bella called Security to get me thrown out," Dominic said with a grin.

"And now you guys are married?" Louis was still trying to wrap his mind around the relationships between the dynamic and intriguing people who were now his family.

"It's a long story," said Bella with a wink. "But the path of true love never did run smooth, isn't that what they say?"

"That's what they say." Louis glanced behind him, hoping to see Sam.

Amado and his wife, Susannah, were there, arms looped around each other's waists, but there was no sign of Sam. She'd slipped away as they'd left Dominic's office, murmuring something about caterers for the party that night.

Since the moment he'd shown up, he'd wanted to take her in his arms. But every time he looked at her, something in her gaze warned him to keep his distance.

"How did you react when Sam first found you?" Fiona picked a clear glass container off one of the polished counters and swirled an imaginary liquid. "Was it a big shock?"

In more ways than you know.

"She'd sent me letters telling me about Tarrant, but I'd ignored them. I guess I wasn't ready. But you can't ignore Sam in person." A grin spread across his mouth.

"Dad sure couldn't." Fiona winked at him. "But I can't complain. As wicked stepmothers go, she's a pretty nice one. How does it feel to have a new, instant stepmom?"

Something in Louis's chest tightened. "I can't think of her that way. She's too young."

Fiona laughed. "That's what they said when she married Dad." She set the glass container down on the counter with a thunk. "But everything's a little different around the Hardcastles, in case you hadn't figured that out already."

Louis could see that Fiona didn't set out to make life easy for Sam. It touched him that Sam was so concerned about building a relationship with the outspoken redhead. *His sister.* Fiona had been Tarrant's only child until recently, and the adjustment must be hard for her. Louis fought the urge to take her in his arms and give her a hug. "Hey, Fiona, how do you feel about suddenly having all these big brothers?"

A wry smile slid across her face. "I always heard that big brothers are great for hooking you up with hot guys. I'm still waiting."

They all laughed. Louis glanced at his brothers, Dominic and Amado. The resemblance between them was striking, unmistakable. There was no doubt they were flesh of the same flesh. Something hot and hard welled up inside him, and emotion threatened to get the better of him.

Brothers.

As a kid he'd sometimes longed for siblings. Someone to share life's dramas and joys with. Suddenly they'd appeared in his life overnight.

"Come on, guys, we've got a lot more to see." Dominic

clapped a hand on Louis's back. "I'm sure Susannah wants to show you the wine cellars she's so painstakingly stocked with the best wine in the world, including her husband's."

"Is that how you two met?" Louis knew that Amado and Susannah were recently married. Romance was apparently thick in the air at Hardcastle Enterprises.

"Susannah came to my estancia in Argentina bearing the news that I might be Tarrant Hardcastle's son."

"Which came as a big shock to him." Susannah shot him a mischievous glance. "Since Amado had been raised to believe his grandparents were his parents. He had no idea his long-dead sister was actually his mother."

"I wasn't all that happy about it, either." Amado gave Louis a wry look. "But Susannah showed me that sometimes having your life turned upside down can be a good thing."

"I agree." Louis looked around at his new family, affection—love—swelling in his heart. "I'm still feeling a little upside down right now. But it's a real good feeling."

Music throbbed over the high-tech sound system and bodies gyrated on the round dance floor cleared in the center of the circular space.

"Fiona," Louis grabbed Fiona as she whirled past him. "Have you seen Sam?"

The pretty redhead glanced around the crowded restaurant.

The party at The Moon, on the top floor of Hardcastle Enterprises' Fifth Avenue headquarters, was supposed to be an intimate gathering of family and close friends. Somehow it had turned into the event of the year, with people jetting in from all over to join the festivities.

Louis wasn't complaining. He loved a good party. Didn't mind being the guest of honor and center of attention, either.

But he was beginning to worry Sam had snuck off to avoid him.

No kiss hello. Not even a polite handshake. Now, wasn't that downright rude?

"I saw her about half an hour ago, fussing over some crusty old friend of Tarrant's who showed up. She's here somewhere, though. She'd never leave a family party."

True. Sam was not the kind of hostess who'd abandon her guests.

Even if she was trying very hard to avoid one of them.

A flash of fine blond hair caught his eye on the far side of the room. Louis excused himself and dived through the elegant crowd. She was chatting with an older woman, and he kept his eyes locked onto her slender back, zipped into a fitted black dress, until he was so close he could smell her expensive scent.

"Sam." He laid his hand on her arm.

She spun around. "Hi, Louis." Her cheery tone was undermined by the panic in her eyes. "Are you enjoying the party?"

"I'm having a wonderful time. There's just one thing missing."

She licked her lips, nervous. "What?"

He leaned in and whispered in her ear. "You."

"I'm sorry, I've been very busy with all the guests." She excused herself from her conversation and the older woman smiled and disappeared into the crowd.

Louis cocked his head. "I'm a guest."

"I asked Dom and Amado to take care of you."

"They did, but now they're both dancing with their wives." He indicated the dance floor with a nod of his head. Dominic swayed to the music, his hands resting on Bella's shapely hips, and Susannah and Amado were locked in a romantic embrace.

"I see what you mean."

"And I don't have a dance partner."

Sam's eyes widened. "I can't... Many of these people are Tarrant's personal friends."

"I'm not asking you to strip naked with me here. Just a friendly dance, that's all."

She stared at him, frozen. Her eyes fell to where his hand still held her slender arm in its firm but gentle grip. "I guess one dance wouldn't hurt."

"You won't even feel a pinch."

A smile crept across his mouth. Without asking, he slid his arm through hers and guided her onto the dance floor.

An inventive DJ was mixing old-school house beats and North African folk music into a pulsing and sultry brew. Dancers swayed and writhed in a fog of sensual heat.

When they reached the center of the crowd, Louis leaned in until his lips almost brushed Sam's ear. "Can you blame me for being hurt that you tracked me down, roped me into a new family, then abandoned me?"

"I'm sure you understand." She started to sway stiffly to the music, standing a good foot away from him.

She looked so nervous and tight. Breathing in shallow gulps and barely able to look at him.

His muscles ached with the desire to take her in his arms. That's what she needed. What they both needed.

But he could see her point. "I do understand. The family you've created here is beautiful. It's powerful, and I can see how you'd do anything to protect it."

She bit her lip again and her eyes welled with tears. "Thank you. It does mean so much to me that you're part of it."

"Me, too." He was surprised by how much emotion he felt meeting his half brothers and half sister. He'd spent the day with them and already felt closer to them than some people he'd known for years. "I feel blessed to have met all of you, no matter how it happened."

Sam's lovely face brightened with a smile that lit the room like rays of sun. Or maybe like the rays of moonlight pouring through the circular skylight open to the stars above.

Then her smile wobbled. "I just wish things had started out differently."

"Maybe you should take the fatalistic approach—that things happen the way they do for a reason."

She frowned, thoughtful. Her body moved more naturally to the music as she got lost in her thoughts, and he tried to keep his eyes from wandering to her breasts or her hips.

"Do you really believe that?"

He sucked in a breath. She deserved his honesty. "Nope. To tell you the truth I think things just happen and you have to deal with them the best you can. I can't think of one single good reason for the city I love to be ravaged by a hurricane." He shrugged. "On the other hand, if it hadn't happened, I'd still be living in Paris."

"You moved back after Katrina?"

"Yes. At first I came to help my grandparents. They were elderly, and the disaster took a big toll on both their health and spirits. Their house had pretty minimal damage since the Quarter stayed dry, so they invited friends to come live with them. I helped sort out meals and beds and all that stuff, and then I got sucked into the magic of the place and its people."

Her blue gaze fixed on his, inviting and encouraging.

"I bought some beautiful old buildings and fixed them up to create new homes for people who'd lost theirs. When things settled down, I helped my granddad rebuild his old boathouse and fishing cabin. By then I knew New Orleans was my home now, not Paris."

Sam had edged closer, probably to hear him over the steady throb of the music. "We read that you've done a lot to help the rebuilding effort."

He frowned. "It feels strange that you guys were researching me when I didn't even know you existed."

She leaned in and he could sense the heat of her skin. "We read about the houses you renovated and the restaurants and bars you opened to create jobs. All that only made us more anxious to meet you. It hurt when you didn't respond to our calls or letters."

A prick of guilt stuck him. He'd dismissed the letters as time-wasting foolishness.

Or had he?

Maybe he'd been afraid of what they might mean.

"I was busy, but perhaps the real reason I didn't respond is that I lost my grandparents last year. They died within a month of each other, and I guess I didn't want to hear or think about any other family right then."

"I'm sorry."

The compassion in her eyes made emotion gather in his chest. "I'm glad I got the opportunity to spend time with them before they passed. That's another blessing that came out of a nightmare."

Dancing had warmed Sam's skin, releasing her scent into the air around them. Her closeness was a delicious torment. All this talk about what he'd lost only made him want to cleave closer to what he'd found.

"You know how it feels to lose someone close."

She looked up. "Like you've lost a part of your own body. It hurts."

"And from what I can see, we both have the same strategy for dealing with the pain. Keep busy."

Sam laughed. A sound that made his heart beat faster. "You're right. I've been like a windup toy since Tarrant died. I try to keep moving every minute of the day."

"You're afraid that if you stop you might fall apart."

Her eyes widened. "Exactly." Then she frowned. "And I don't want to fall apart. I've had enough drama and crisis in my life over the last decade. I'd rather lift my chin up and keep dancing. Does that sound crazy?"

Sympathy swelled in his heart. "Not at all. It sounds brave."

Her strength of spirit moved him, and the desire to take her in his arms became a steady ache, throbbing in time to the lilting and sensual music that filled the air around them.

"We're a lot alike, you and I, Sam," he whispered into her ear, leaning close. "I think we're both most comfortable in a crowd, surrounded by laughter and chatter and people having a good time. Or even people pretending to have a good time."

She looked up at him, blue eyes sparkling. "We're people people."

He chuckled. "Yes. And sometimes it's easier for us to spend our time greasing the social wheels so we don't have to think about what we truly want."

Emotion flickered in the depths of her eyes. She bit her lip.

He inched toward her, enjoying the heat of her skin through her stiff black dress. "Or about what we *need*."

He'd had enough of her no-touching routine. Right now he needed to hold her more than he'd ever needed anything. "Come with me."

He grasped her hand and she didn't fight him. Slowly, without betraying the urgency he felt, he led her through the crowd of gyrating bodies and toward the exit.

She didn't protest as he led her past the uniformed waiters

handing parting gifts to the guests. Or even when he ushered her into a waiting elevator.

The doors closed leaving them alone for the first time since his arrival in New York. His lips and hands fought the urge to take hold of her and kiss some sense into her.

A glance up at the ubiquitous security camera restrained him.

Sam looked at him, nervous and expectant, as they stepped out into the silent lobby. She muttered a nervous goodbye to the security guard at the desk.

Outside the elegant Hardcastle building that took up most of a Fifth Avenue block, lamplight created pools of golden light in the darkness. "We'll go to my hotel," he murmured, shielding his voice from the scattered passersby. "It's only two blocks away."

Sam didn't protest. She kept stride with him in the warm fall air. "I wonder what they'll say when they realize I've gone."

"I hate to say it, but they're probably all having too much fun to notice."

Her pained expression made him regret his words.

She looked away. "You're right, of course. I sometimes get an exaggerated sense of my own importance. I forget everyone else has a full life of their own to occupy their time." Her voice shook and he felt her hand cool in his.

Louis stopped walking, spun in front of her and took both her hands. "You are important. You're the reason we're all here tonight. Your energy and vision and heart made it happen. And you're important to me." He said the words with force. He felt so much more than he could put into mere words.

As her delicate pink mouth quivered, no doubt preparing a rebuttal, he leaned in and kissed her.

Her lips parted and welcomed his mouth to hers. His arms instinctively slid around her waist and he held her against him, kissing her with all the painful longing he'd stored up over the past days and nights.

A shudder rippled through her, the force of her relief so strong he could feel it like an electric jolt. She was every bit as hungry and desperate for this kiss as he was.

Finally the synapses of his brain started firing again and he managed to pull back. Sam blinked like an animal startled out of its burrow. Her mouth opened to speak, but no words came out.

"We'd better keep walking." He slid his arm through hers. "We're nearly there."

Sam put on dark glasses when they approached the entrance to the elegant hotel.

"Shades at night?" Louis couldn't resist teasing. "Worried the lobby lights will be too bright?"

"I could run into someone I know."

"So? We're not doing anything criminal."

She glanced at him. The wide, black lenses hid her eyes, but the muscles in her jaw were rigid. "Maybe not criminal, but...*scandalous*." The final word came out as a whisper.

Truth be told, it shot a bolt of lust right through him. Apparently the scandal thing just didn't get under his skin the way it did with Sam.

But he respected her wish for privacy.

He guided her across the shimmering marble floor of the hotel lobby, enjoying the elegant sashay of her tight behind as she walked in front of him. The prospect of seeing her naked in his bed again made his skin hum with excitement.

She stood in the back of the elevator, dark glasses still covering her beautiful eyes, while the doors closed.

"I think the sunglasses make you look like you have something to hide."

"I do."

"At least you can't hide it from me." Again, only the security camera made him keep his hands off her luscious body, pressed so enticingly against the marble wall of the elevator.

His fingers stung with anticipation as he unlocked the door and ushered her in. He'd ordered champagne and caviar at the front desk and it was already being delivered when he and Sam arrived at the room. He tipped the waiter and ushered Sam inside.

Heat flared through him as the door closed behind him with a click.

"I do hate eating caviar off dry saltines. A beautiful woman's naked body is so much more *sympathique*."

"You're wicked." She lowered the glasses to reveal a mischievous gleam in her own eyes.

"With my wild upbringing, how could I not be? Take pity on me anyway." He cocked his head and allowed a grin to slip across his mouth.

"Apparently I can't help myself."

Somehow they'd already drifted together and his hands found their way to her hips. Her dress was black and structured, and hid the soft curves of her body under taut seams and crisp peaks of fabric. "We need to get this off."

His voice came out a little huskier than he intended, but his request had the desired effect. Sam nodded and started to struggle with a zipper buried in a side seam.

Louis's arousal thickened as he tugged the zipper pull along the hourglass curve of her waist and snuck a fingerful of silky skin on his way down.

Sam wriggled under his touch and a soft moan escaped her

mouth. Together they struggled with the stiff silk, tugging it down over her pert breasts, past her slim hips and over her sweet, tight ass.

"Much better," he breathed, when she stepped out of it. Now she wore nothing but a skimpy black lace bra and panties.

She blushed. "I hate panty hose in summer."

"Me, too. All that nylon makes my legs itch."

Sam giggled. Her eyes zeroed in on his crotch, which hardened when she reached for the button on his pants and boldly unfastened it.

With careful concentration, she unzipped and pushed the fabric down over his thighs and calves. "I'm going to have to take my shoes off," he said, as the touch of her soft fingers on his skin almost deprived him of rational thought.

"Oh, yeah. Let me unlace them."

The view from above, as she crouched to unlace his shoes, was magnificent. Her delicate panties only had a slim string in the back, revealing her well-exercised backside in all its taut perfection.

Sam turned her attention to the buttons of his shirt, pressing her thighs to his as she unbuttoned them. Louis grew as hard as the bedrock under Manhattan.

He couldn't keep his hands off her. Her slender body was an enticing combination of soft curves and strong muscle. His fingers roamed over her smooth, warm skin, reveling in all the sensations he'd missed during their agonizing evening of no touching.

Sam's fingers shook as she struggled with the buttons. Her breath came in unsteady gasps. Her urgency was palpable.

Which gave him a wicked idea.

"You know, Sam," he murmured, watching her fingers undo the last button and push the shirt back over his shoulders.

"What?" She didn't look up from her task. Apparently she was too engrossed in pushing the rumpled broadcloth down over his arms.

"I think maybe you were right."

"Right about what?" She fumbled with one of the cuffs, which was buttoned.

"Maybe we shouldn't touch each other."

Now she looked up. Her blue eyes narrowed. "You're kidding."

The shirt, hung up on that last button, came free and fell to the floor, leaving him dressed only in a pair of boxers that did absolutely nothing to hide his intense arousal.

The look of sudden desperation on her face almost made him reconsider.

But not quite.

She'd put him through the hell of keeping his hands off her, when he wanted nothing more than to take her in his arms and hold her.

Let's see how she liked it when the tables were turned.

"I obeyed your rules when you decided we shouldn't touch." He cocked his head. "Now I think it's only fair that you obey mine. Don't you agree?"

She licked her lips. Her nipples had tightened to rosy peaks beneath her transparent bra and her belly trembled visibly with arousal.

"Why?" she rasped.

"For fun." He let a naughty grin slide across his mouth. "Go lie on the bed."

It was a command, not a question.

She peered at him for a second, then crossed the room with elegant strides. He couldn't peel his eyes off the delicious view of her backside in its provocative underwear.

Mrs. Hardcastle clearly had a wild streak that she kept very firmly under designer wraps.

He was going to make it growl.

She eased onto the bed on her stomach, all lithe tan curves and thinly veiled enthusiasm.

"I don't know if I can trust you," he said, standing over her so that the light cast his shadow on her skin.

He wasn't sure he could trust himself, either. But it would be fun trying.

"I'll be good." She blinked innocently.

"If you're not, then do I have the right to take appropriate corrective measures?"

She peered at him, mischief sparkling in her eyes. "Of course."

"Excellent. I can see we understand each other." He walked to the table where the champagne sat cooling in a silver ice bucket. He poured a single flute.

He walked back to the bed, carrying it between his thumb and forefinger. "Since we're avoiding touch, we'll explore the other senses. First, taste."

He held out the glass. "I want you to take a sip." She reached for it. "Don't swallow any of it. Just take the champagne into your mouth and enjoy the taste of it. Then, you'll pass it to me."

"Without touching?" She looked doubtful.

"Not even a tiny brush of skin."

Wary blue eyes on him, she rose onto her knees and took the glass—avoiding his fingers with care—and took a sip. He watched her face as the bubbles tickled over her tongue.

Louis climbed on the bed, careful to keep a few inches between them, which was a challenge given the movement of the mattress.

He lay on his back and maneuvered his head between her parted legs. The scent of her silky skin wrapped around him. *Just who was he trying to torment, here?*

Sam leaned forward, a cautious smile on her face, her cheeks slightly swollen with champagne. She poised her mouth about an inch over his—which nearly killed him—and he opened his mouth so that she could drip the champagne into it.

Warm and sweet from her mouth, the sparkling liquid felt like a taste of heaven on Louis's parched tongue. Only one drop spilled and rolled over his chin.

He swallowed and licked his lips. "Thanks."

Sam grinned. He saw her glance down at his shorts, where his intense arousal must be very evident.

"Name another sense."

"Um," she bit her luscious pink lip. "How about hearing?" She narrowed her eyes, apparently doubtful that he could manage it.

"Excellent choice. You're going to listen to my heart rate while I tell you some of the things I could be doing to you right now."

Her eyes widened.

"Lie on your side." He waited for her to shift to one side of the bed, then he positioned himself alongside her, so his chest was level with her head. "Come close," he whispered. "But remember, touching has its consequences, so be careful."

She edged toward him, bracing herself on the soft mattress with manicured fingertips, wary as a hunter. She paused an inch or two from his chest, tucking her silky hair behind her ear. A diamond glittered in her soft, pink lobe and he fought a sudden urge to forget this stupid game and just kiss her.

"Oh, my gosh," she exclaimed. "I can hear your heartbeat and it just sped up!"

Louis grunted. This whole stunt might reveal too much about him to a woman who obviously had way too much power over him. He was pretty on edge after all the emotion of the day and the excitement of meeting his new siblings.

"Go on, do tell. I want to know what revs your engine." Sam grinned, clearly relishing his disadvantage.

"You do," he growled.

"So I see. And I want to hear exactly what you'd like to do to me." Her blue gaze challenged him to lie to her.

Louis stretched a little, causing her to pull back a bit or risk touching him with her cheek. "First, I'd like to trace my tongue all the way from your glittering earlobe, down your sensitive neck, to your nipples."

"Oh, yeah, faster still."

Her grin irked him. "I'd like to undo your bra with my teeth."

She raised a brow. "This one has a tricky hook."

"I have talented teeth."

"Ooh." Her dimple grew deeper. "Then what?"

"I'd like to lick your nipples until they grow hard."

"Won't take long."

"Then trail my tongue over your belly and down past your waist, until I reach the top of your thighs…"

"Your pulse is thumping."

"I'll bet." Louis could barely think. His blood had departed his brain for lower regions, which throbbed painfully. "And then…all right, enough of this one." He rolled off the bed, away from her.

Whose dumb idea was this?

Sam's eyes shone. "Which sense is next?"

She was enjoying this far too much. She was supposed to be the one suffering.

"How about smell?" she continued. She'd flipped onto her back and lay supine, arms behind her head, giving him a dangerously enticing view of her gorgeous body. "I'd like to smell you. All over."

Louis gave her a funny look. "I don't know if that's a good idea. It's been a long day."

"All the better. Come on. It's not fair for you to have all the fun."

"All right, knock yourself out." Louis eased himself back onto the soft covers. At the very least, this should diminish his agonizing arousal.

At least that's what he thought until Sam climbed over him.

"Hey, wait, your hair's touching me." The fine strands brushed his chest like butterfly wings, making his skin twitch.

"Doesn't count." Sam leaned closer. Her hair brushed higher as her nose sought out his neck, then his cheek.

Worse than the silky fall on his chest was the fact that he could smell *her*. The familiar French scent blended exquisitely with her own delicately erotic, feminine fragrance. The result was magic, like a thousand-dollar bottle of wine, the perfect freshly dug truffle or the finest handmade Swiss chocolate.

Did her husband choose that scent for her?

His *father?*

His muscles knotted and he jerked up. Their cheeks clashed and his chest collided with hers.

"What?" She sprang back.

"Enough," he growled. "This is killing me."

"It was your idea."

"I'm an idiot."

She shot him a sympathetic look, but excitement danced

in her eyes. "But you still have to pay the consequences, so it's only fair if you tell me what you were going to do to me if I touched you."

Oh, yes. He'd been right about that wild streak. Desire flashed through him. He'd unleashed the real Sam, the energetic and creative person who'd kept quiet and played nice all those years.

She excited him more than any woman he'd ever met, and his desire for her stung his veins and drove him half mad.

To complicate matters, they were already "family"—in the most unconventional way—so there was no disappearing over the horizon when the party ended.

But he didn't care. They were on this adventure together and he intended to strap in and enjoy the ride, wherever it took them.

Even if it meant letting her tie him up.

Seven

Sam laughed at the look on his face. Cocky and apprehensive. She wouldn't have thought those two could go together.

But she'd never met a man like Louis before.

"Go on, spill." She leaned in, giving him a view of her cleavage that attracted his eyes like a hypnotist's pendulum. "What should I do with you?"

She probably should be surprised by the flirty tone in her voice, or by the way she kept edging closer just to torment him, but for reasons she couldn't explain she felt totally... *comfortable.*

"Well." He licked his lip, which caused a pleasurable throb between her legs. "I had intended to tie you—very gently—to the bedpost so I could have my wicked way with you."

A rakish smile crossed his mouth.

"Ooh. Sounds like fun. I'm sorry I'll miss out." She pressed a finger thoughtfully to her lip. "Now, what shall I tie you with?"

"Your bra." He seemed to be struggling to tug his eyes away from it. In fact, his obvious appreciation for her entire body was more arousing than she could have imagined.

Under his gaze she felt powerfully female and desirable, maybe for the first time in her whole life. "What was that you said about your talented teeth?"

He raised a dark brow. "Is this some kind of dare?"

"Absolutely." She thrust her breasts under his chin. His obvious pleasure in her action only encouraged her to wriggle a little under his gaze. "I'm waiting."

"I don't think I can do it without touching," he rasped, eyes still riveted on her breasts.

"Touching is okay, just no hands."

Her skin craved his touch with an intensity that made her body sparkle with anticipation.

Louis eyed the clasp in front of her bra like a jewel thief studying a challenging safe combination.

Sam managed not to squirm as his face lowered between her breasts and he closed his mouth over the clasp of her bra. His lips brushed her skin and sheer pleasure shivered through her. Her nipples hummed at his nearness, and in anticipation of being freed from their lacy cage.

In about three seconds, Louis had the clasp undone. He looked up, triumph gleaming in his eyes.

"That's some talent." She slid the bra down her arms and dangled it from her fingertips. "Now come on over to the bedpost."

Louis eased his muscled body across the bed, and she bound one hand to the polished mahogany by winding her bra around it a few times and fastening the clasp. He would have no problem wiggling free if he wasn't man enough to stand up to his own challenge.

But she had a feeling Louis didn't back down on a promise.

She began by layering floaty kisses over his stomach, then his thighs. Just as it looked as if his shorts might burst at the seams, she pulled them down and let him spring free.

Her own excitement made her giggle more than once. It was torture to be so close to making love with this man, yet to keep delaying it.

But it was so much fun.

Sam wasn't sure she'd ever actually had *fun* in bed with a man before.

Tarrant hadn't been able to…well, get it up, for want of a less blunt description.

And she hadn't minded. Really, she hadn't. Her first two marriages had left her with the impression that sex was a tiresome marital obligation in the same category as starching and ironing shirts, and it was a relief not to have to do either for Tarrant.

Last time with Louis had been intense and explosive, but too edged with her own desperation to be described as "fun."

This was totally different.

Louis knew all about her. About her past relationships and the experiences that had made her who she was. There was nothing to hide from him. She could think about her former husbands right now, as she hovered over his dangerously aroused body, and not feel guilty or ashamed about anything. She didn't have to fake innocence or experience she didn't have in order to be "perfect."

He'd invited her to be herself, and told her that was all he wanted.

Now here she was. All her usual doubts and fears and

worries were still there, but they didn't seem that big and important anymore.

Which made licking his skin and enjoying his warm, male scent all the more enjoyable.

"You know you're killing me." Louis's pained expression was undermined by the glitter of pleasure in his eyes.

"I never knew I had such a taste for murder." She looked up from kissing his belly. His arousal was so raw and visible, it made her heart jump in her chest.

He was this excited about being here with *her*.

His strong, young, muscled body was having a pretty dramatic effect on her libido, too. She'd never seen a more beautiful physique.

Athletic, but not in the heavy, gym-pumped manner of a bodybuilder. More natural and sexy. His tan skin was smooth, which made it glow in the warm light from the bedside lamp.

As she tormented him with her lips and tongue, she enjoyed watching his muscles tense and tighten as he tried to keep control.

"Sam." His guttural voice betrayed his urgency. His free hand fisted into the sheets and the bound one strained against her flimsy bra.

The bra snapped.

Louis flinched when the elastic smacked his wrist. He rubbed it, then looked up at her with a predatory grin.

Sam's whole body convulsed in an involuntary shiver. The next thing she knew she was climbing over him, clawing at his skin and pressing herself against him.

Louis's arms circled her waist and she let out a shuddering sigh as he gathered her into his hot and hungry embrace.

"You don't know how much I've craved this," she murmured.

"Yes," he replied, breath warm on her ear. "I do."

In less than a second he was inside her, filling her with all the desire and longing and hope she knew she'd created in him. It was blissful agony to finally give into the yearnings she'd tried so hard—and failed—to master.

They rolled on the sheets, switching roles, enjoying each other's bodies with abandon. The pleasurable sensations grew so intense and overwhelming that Sam heard herself laugh out loud.

Louis's obvious delight in her pleasure only heightened it. He kissed and caressed her, touched her with tenderness that made her heart flutter, then groped her in rough excitement that made her pulse throb faster and her breath come in unsteady gasps.

Her orgasm blew out of nowhere like a tornado on a clear day. It whirled her around—twisting and turning and picking up cows and houses and the roofs of strip malls—then flung her down on the rumpled sheets in a heap, unable to move or even speak, her limbs weighted with blissful relief.

She opened her eyes to see Louis next to her, chest heaving with exertion. His closed-eyed expression had a strange intensity to it, like someone deep in meditation.

"You okay?" she rasped.

"Very much so." The smile appeared around the edges of his sensual mouth, then his eyes slit open, sparkling gold. "Aren't you glad you finally got some sense and came to my bed?"

"Yes," she admitted. "I'm honestly not sure how I'll feel in the morning, but right now I'm very glad to be here."

He slid his palm over her belly and let it lie there, warm and reassuring. "Just take it one minute at a time."

She drew in a deep breath and let it out. "I'll try."

Louis nuzzled close, resting his nose and mouth in the

crook of her neck, where they fit perfectly, his breath soft on her skin.

What a relief not to have to fill the air with false promises and phony reassurances. Around Louis it was okay to be confused and uncertain. To be truthful. Maybe if she spent enough time with him, she really would be able to figure out who she was and actually have a shot at "being herself."

With that rather exciting thought floating around her brain, Sam drifted off to a peaceful sleep.

"Room service" were the first words Sam heard on waking the next morning. They were coming from the other side of the door and they barely penetrated her consciousness, but she still gathered enough sense to pull the sheets over most of her head and freeze in a panic.

Did Louis not care if people saw them together? It was one thing for them to enjoy intimacy in private, but quite another for the rest of New York to find out about it.

She heard Louis exchange pleasantries with the waiter, and when the door clicked, she emerged. "You could have warned me," she murmured, pushing hair out of her eyes.

"You looked so peaceful, I couldn't bear to wake you. And I'm starving." His mischievous grin melted her pique.

"I can believe it. You were pretty athletic last night." She blew out a breath, remembering some of the Kama-Sutra-style moves he'd introduced her to. Her insides shimmered at the memory.

"So I need some ham and eggs."

"I'm surprised. That seems very traditional for you."

"Every now and then I even surprise myself. I ordered plenty for you, too, and a basket of breads and pastries. We can call down for anything else you want."

The smell of freshly baked brioche tickled Sam's nostrils. "I'm sure I can manage with what you ordered." Suddenly she was starving, too. She glanced around for something to wear, then remembered she had nothing but her rather uncomfortable little black dress from last night.

"Here," Louis winked and threw her a robe with the hotel logo emblazoned on the pocket.

"Thanks," she rasped, and pulled it on. She scanned the room for mirrors. "I'm sure I look pretty scary."

"You look devastating, as usual." Louis helped himself to a heaping plate of ham and eggs. He wore only a pair of cream-colored cotton pajama pants, and his bare, muscled chest made an attractive backdrop for the feast now spread on the table.

Sam's stomach grumbled and she climbed over the bed. Louis abandoned his plate long enough to kiss her good morning. Her insides buckled at the soft touch of his lips on hers.

"Oh, goodness. What a night." She smiled shyly at him.

"What a night." He smiled back. "Now help yourself to some food and rebuild your strength."

Sam chose a croissant and spread it with butter. Her personal trainer would have a heart attack at the sight of so much cholesterol, but if you were going wild, then why not go all the way?

Louis poured her a cup of coffee and she took an invigorating sip. A stack of newspapers rested on the far side of the table, and she wandered over to glance at the headlines. *The New York Times* newspaper was on top with an article about a corporate bigwig she knew slightly who'd apparently been nailed for tax evasion.

She shook her head. How could smart people be so stupid? She lifted the *Times* to see what was underneath.

Merry Widow Makes Out.

Her heart froze at the sight of the tabloid's familiar moniker—for her. She grabbed the paper and managed to focus her eyes on the grainy black-and-white image underneath the headline.

"Oh, no." She could make out a blurry outline of herself and Louis, locked in an embrace. The one clear and unmistakable thing in the photo was her face, lit up against the darkness, eyes closed in an expression of rapture.

Her legs grew shaky and she reached for a chair.

"What's going on?" Louis looked up from a sip of coffee. At the sight of her face, he rose from his chair and moved around the table.

He took the paper from her hand and muttered a curse when he saw the headline and picture. "That's not right."

Sam's temples started to throb. "I should be used to it by now." She shook her head. "But at least in the past, it was all lies and innuendo. Now they actually have a story."

"Do they know who I am?" Louis scanned the paper. "Damn."

"They do?"

"Yeah. I'm your 'handsome stepson.'"

Sam pushed her face into her hands. She didn't want to see anything. She could feel the walls closing in on her as her delicately ordered world began to crumble.

She was dimly aware of Louis crouching down next to her chair. "Sam, I'm sorry this happened."

"Me, too," she breathed, her words barely audible.

"I mean, I'm not sorry I kissed you. I'm sorry those idiots made a story out of it." She felt his hand on her spine, rubbing gently.

Her back stiffened. "I'm sorry about both."

She turned to face him, angry at herself and angry at him, too, for letting her do something so stupid.

She reached for the paper and Louis pulled it back. "Why read it?"

"Because I need to know what's being said." She heard the same clipped tones she used when her assistant, Kelly, tried to keep the morning papers away from her on one pretext or other.

Louis handed her the paper and she scanned the lines.

Speculation has it that the widow isn't content with the mere millions she inherited from late retail tycoon Tarrant Hardcastle, and that she wants to get her manicured fingers on the rumored billions stashed away for his heirs. If this kiss is any indication, she's struck the jackpot.

Sam let out a fierce growl. "Ugh! How do they come up with this stuff? It was my idea to have Tarrant set aside money for his heirs."

Louis took the paper and read it, then shook his head. "They're mad at you because you're young, beautiful and rich. Simple jealousy. You can't let it get to you."

"Trust me, I try not to, but this time it's my fault."

"Because you kissed me?"

"Because I kissed anyone out on a public street in New York. I must be losing my mind. Right on Fifth Avenue." She shook her head in disbelief at her own stupidity.

He was a grown-up, too, and old enough to know better, even if he was her *handsome stepson*.

She cringed and hurried around the bed, looking for her dress. She shook it out and stepped into it, then crammed her bare feet into her high black stilettos.

"I guess everyone out there will know I unexpectedly stayed the night somewhere anyway, so no big deal trying to look decent."

She didn't like the bitterness in her voice, but she couldn't help the way she felt. How could she have been so stupid as to hand her head on a stake to the tabloid press?

Fiona would see it.

And Dominic and Amado.

All the staff at Hardcastle Enterprises.

Not to mention her personal staff at home.

Her face burned with shame and tears pricked her eyes.

"I wish I could do something to make it all go away," said Louis softly.

"You can't." The angry shrew voice sprang from her mouth again. "Gee, I thought New Orleans had all that old black magic and voodoo stuff. I'd think a carefully laid curse here and there—maybe a couple of stringer reporters turning into toads—wouldn't be too much to ask."

Louis shot her a pained smile.

"I guess that would be bad for my karma or something. Not that it could make much difference, really. How much worse can it get?"

"Sam, calm down. Nothing has actually happened. No one's hurt, no one's died. Put it in perspective." Louis stood in front of her, sculpted arms hanging by his sides, his handsome face set in an expression of easy confidence.

She hated the fact that heat flashed over her—even now, when arousal should be the very last thing on her mind.

The unwelcome desire morphed into a kind of crazed fury. "Nothing has happened?" she spat the question at him. "I'm hurt. You're hurt."

She paused, gasping for breath. "And Tarrant has died. If

he hadn't died, none of this would have happened. Why did he have to die?"

The last part emerged on a wail. She grabbed her dark glasses off the table and tears blinded her as she rushed for the door.

"Sam, wait." She heard Louis's voice behind her while she struggled with the knob and crashed out into the hall. "Sam."

She cringed at the sound of his voice calling down the hall as she stood waiting for the elevator, then the doors opened and she stepped in.

In the elevator she tried her best to fix her hair in the reflection on the mirrored walls. She adjusted her big sunglasses over her tear-filled eyes. Then she breathed in as deeply as she could and prepared to face the worst humiliation of her life.

Eight

Sam could hear her cell vibrating in her clutch purse on the side table.

Or maybe it was just the whole mansion vibrating with distress.

The staff slunk along the walls, trying to be invisible. No one would look her in the eye. Except Fiona.

"How could you do this?" Her stepdaughter's face was blotchy and pale. "I mean, he's my brother! That's just sick." Her pretty features contorted with disgust.

Sam's gut twisted. "It was an accident."

Fiona blew out a snort. "Good one. Try again."

Sam shoved a hand through her tangled hair. "I had no idea who he was when I met him. I didn't even know his name."

"And you thought it would be a good idea to sleep with him?" Fiona scowled. "Jeez, and don't I remember you giving me a maternal lecture about choosing my partners carefully just a few months ago? I guess it's *Do as I say, not as I do.*"

Sam felt tears prick her throat. She'd tried so hard to be a good role model for Fiona, whose own mother was a preoccupied socialite with little time for her "plain" daughter.

It had taken her three full years to gain Fiona's trust, and they'd bonded even more closely since Tarrant's death. She'd cried on Fiona's shoulder more than once in the emotional aftermath, and she'd come to think of her as a younger sister.

Now their hard-won relationship lay in ruins.

Fiona glanced over her shoulder at Sam's bag. "I think your phone is ringing."

"I'm so, so sorry."

"Don't apologize to me. It's not even my business." Fiona crossed her arms over her green T-shirt. "But that buzzing is driving me nuts. Are you afraid to answer it in case it's the press? There must be twenty of them gathered on the front steps."

Sam froze. "You're kidding."

"Didn't Beatrice tell you?"

"No." The housekeeper had been avoiding her glance as if she couldn't even stand to look at her. "Is it just newspapers or are there TV cameras, too?"

Fiona cocked her head. "Why? Want to know what kind of direction to give your makeup artist?"

Irritation flared in Sam's chest. "Fiona, did you leak this to the press?"

Fiona cocked her head. "Do you really think I would do that?"

"You're the one that leaked the story about Dominic and Bella, aren't you? No one else could have known the details."

The younger woman froze.

Anger and hurt rose in Sam's chest. "I've tried so hard to be a friend to you, Fiona. I do think you've had a raw deal around here and I can see why you feel sidelined by all these new siblings you never asked for. But it's not fair to try and destroy other people's lives as revenge."

Red blotches stood out on Fiona's pale face. "I admit, I did leak the story about Dominic and Bella. I was so mad! Dominic came out of nowhere and suddenly Dad's all dewy-eyed and can't wait to hand over the whole empire to him. I felt invisible. But I swear I didn't say anything about you and Louis. How could I? I had no idea." Her voice cracked with desperation—and what sounded like honesty.

"Really?"

"Really. Who on earth would imagine you, little Mrs. Goody Two-shoes, would be shacking up with her own stepson?"

Sam gulped. "You have a point."

"And Sam—" Fiona swallowed "—I really do like you. You've been so kind to me, even though I've tried my best to make you hate me. Sad as it is, you're probably the best friend I have." Fiona's lip quivered.

Sam's heart squeezed. "I like you, too, Fiona. I really do. Oh, dear. What are we going to do now? Is it just local press?"

"It's national. You'd better pull yourself together. You're not looking your best. Breath mint?" Fiona pulled a tube of mints from her pocket and held it up.

Sam shook her head, but the strange humor of the gesture gave her a slim ray of hope that all was not lost. "I don't think a breath mint could do much for me now. I'm just going to barricade myself in the way I usually do." She paused and rubbed her eyes. "And believe me when I say that if I could undo what I did…"

"Well, you can't. But that's life, isn't it?" Fiona winked. "Honestly, it's a bit of a relief that you're not such a freaking saint after all. You're always so loving and giving and generous, with time for everyone, and never a hair out of place." She cast a glance at Sam's hair and chuckled. "Guess you're human after all."

The phone started to buzz again.

"If you don't get that, I will." Fiona started across the room.

Adrenaline flashed through Sam and she rushed after her. "I'll get it!"

"Afraid it's lover boy?"

Yes.

"It could be Dominic or Amado calling to find out what the fuss is about." She hadn't faced them yet, since they didn't live with her in the Park Avenue mansion like Fiona.

She shoved a hand into her purse and pulled out the vibrating instrument. "Hello."

"Hey, Sam." The soft, deep voice seemed to reach right out of the dark metal and caress her ear.

She recoiled from the sensation and her finger hovered over the disconnect button.

"It's him, isn't it?" Fiona stared at her, emerald eyes narrowed.

Sam nodded. "Hello," she croaked.

Part of her wished he'd just disappear to Europe, or even New Orleans, at least until this whole thing blew over. And part of her wished he was right here, holding her in his strong arms.

"How're you holding up?"

"I'm okay," she said, trying to convince herself. "I'm with Fiona. I think she's beginning to see the humor in the situation." She risked a cautious glance at Fiona.

Fiona shot her a little smirk.

"Not that it's actually funny, of course," she backtracked. "It's horribly embarrassing. The staff is avoiding me like I have bird flu. Tarrant's housekeeper has been with him for twenty years and I think she'd be glad to throw me out to the reporters."

"I'm watching TV," Louis interrupted. "They're broadcasting from the steps of your mansion."

Fear shot through Sam. "Right now?"

"Yes, there's a woman with apricot helmet-hair telling the story of your life."

"Oh, no." Heat flooded her face. She glanced at the windows, suddenly afraid helicopters might be hovering outside, looking to snap her picture.

They'd love that. She'd probably never looked worse. It would be a great "where are they now" shot in contrast with her old beauty queen pictures.

Sam cursed herself for the vain thought. "I'm just going to sit tight. They swarmed around right after Tarrant's death, when the news came out that he'd left me so much money, but eventually they got bored and went away."

"How long did that take?"

She rubbed her temples. "A couple of weeks."

"You're going to stay locked up in that house for two whole weeks? Besides, it could be longer this time. It's a juicier story." A hint of innuendo colored his voice.

Oh, boy, is it ever.

"Staying inside for a few days is no big deal."

She heard a snort of disbelief. "Sam, you can't let them keep you prisoner."

"Really, I have everything I need. There's a staff of fifteen."

"I'm coming over."

The conviction in his voice warmed her heart for a split second, then adrenaline rocketed through her veins. "Please, don't! You'll only make it worse. They'll be all over you. You have no idea of the kinds of things they'll say to make a story."

"I can handle myself."

"Louis, please." She sucked in a deep breath. "I hate to say it, since I brought you here to meet the family, but I think you should leave town. At least for a while."

"Sweetheart, I'm not going to let anyone run me out of town, least of all you." Humor deepened his voice.

Sam found herself wanting to smile. But it wasn't a laughing matter. "It might hurt your business. Restaurants are all about image and perception."

"And food. Are you eating? I bet you're not."

Sam glanced down at her stomach. She'd run from the hotel room before her first bite of croissant and since she'd been back at the mansion she hadn't even taken off the awful black dress from last night.

"Give me Fiona."

"What?"

"You heard me." Louis's tone brooked no contradiction.

Sam stared at the phone for a moment, frowning, then held it out to Fiona.

Fiona looked alarmed, but extended a pale, rather shaky hand and took it. "Hello?" she said slowly.

Sam rubbed her hands over her face. She felt quite light-headed. She really should eat. What on earth was he saying to Fiona? She could hear the low murmur of his voice on the other end of the phone.

Fiona listened with total concentration, nodding silently. She chewed her lip. "Are you sure that's a good idea?" she asked at last.

Sam's stomach knotted. "Sure what's a good idea?"

She could hear Louis's murmur again.

After a few seconds, she handed the phone back to Sam, who rushed it to her ear only to hear the grim drone of the dial tone. "He doesn't say goodbye politely on the phone," she muttered, remembering the time he'd hung up after issuing orders on what she should wear for dinner.

"No." Fiona grinned.

"What are you smiling at?"

"Nothing."

"Then stop it." She couldn't help smiling, mostly because she was immensely relieved to see Fiona smiling, too.

"Can't. You know, you really look *awful*." Fiona tilted her head as if to get a better angle on Sam's shocking awfulness. "I wouldn't have believed it possible. You're not even all that pretty without your makeup on. You have these funny little dark splotches under your eyes. Your hair looks like straw, and your nose is bright red, like a circus clown." She let out a laugh.

Sam's hand flew self-consciously to the straw. "So glad I can provide some comic relief at this moment of high drama."

"Yeah." Fiona chuckled. "I love it. Usually I feel like such a dumpy klutz around you. Little did I know the whole effect was painted on."

Sam put her hands on her hips. "I should be offended."

"Yeah." Fiona pressed a thoughtful finger to her lips. "You know, you really should let the press get a look at you right now. I bet they'd stop being so mean."

"Maybe I'll go to the door right now and weep all over them."

"Nah. Don't give 'em the satisfaction." Fiona slid her arm around Sam's shoulders. "We'd better get you fixed up before Louis gets here."

"He's truly coming?" Panic rippled over her.

"Of course he is. Did you have any doubt?"

"We've got to stop him."

Fiona laughed, as if Sam had suggested trying to turn back the tide. "Let's go get you something to eat."

Louis marched along Park Avenue with determination surging through him like liquor. Sam *needed* him. And not as a stepson, either.

Thick clusters of pink coneflowers and yellow black-eyed Susans bloomed their hearts out in steel planters along the facade of a tall office block. Their honeyed smell rose into the hot air, propelling him faster toward Sam.

Every moment they spent together, he could see her opening up like a flower, shedding the molds she'd crammed herself into in the past and finally transforming into the glorious, powerful woman who'd been crouching inside all along.

Even here in the concrete-covered heart of one of the largest cities on earth, bees buzzed around the plump centers of the flowers, gathering pollen to make the delicious honey that sustained them.

Louis felt like a bee around Sam, drinking in all her powerful energy and refreshing his own life force by helping her rediscover hers.

He laughed aloud. He could intellectualize it all he wanted; the truth was they'd had *great* sex together.

He pulled open his cell and punched in a number. A female voice answered.

"Margo, it's Louis."

"Hi, baby," her rich voice greeted him. "Are you coming up to New York for my opening next week?"

"I wouldn't miss it for anything, and I've found you a new student."

"Hmm, let me guess, she's brilliant and beautiful and you're on a mission to help her find herself."

He frowned. "Am I that predictable?"

"Yes," she chuckled. "But you're lovable, too."

Louis shoved a hand through his hair. Okay, so he'd dated a few wealthy and beautiful women who needed help finding themselves. But somehow the idea that Sam was another in his long string of lovely ex-girlfriends scratched at someplace uncomfortable inside him.

He marched faster along the street. "Sam's different. She's been through a lot. She's going to need all your encouragement just to overcome her self-doubt."

"Ah, a project. And who'll be mopping up her tears when you run off to Paris or Milan and don't call when you said you would? What was it you said last time? 'Every relationship has its season'?"

"That sounds like something my mother would say."

"You're more like her than you'll admit."

Louis dodged to avoid a cab speeding through a red light. "I am not."

"Oh, yes, you are, sweetie. Sipping the nectar from each pretty flower, then moving on."

Louis froze at her use of the metaphor he'd just been contemplating himself. He hated when the universe locked onto him like that. "The bee plays a valuable role in pollination. Bringing each flower to life." He shoved a hand through his hair as he resumed his marching.

He didn't say that since he'd met Sam, he found himself contemplating the deeper and more fulfilling pleasures of sticking around to make honey.

"My new student, is she madly in love with you?"

Louis stopped dead in the middle of the Park Avenue sidewalk. A rushing man in a suit slammed into him from behind and they muttered apologies.

"No, she's not."

"Or at least that's what you're telling yourself so you don't feel so bad when you leave her for the next pretty project."

Her comment cut to his heart. Sam was so different from anyone he'd ever met. "Margo, I'm going to stop inviting you to my restaurants."

"No, you won't. You love my refreshing honesty."

Louis laughed. Then he caught sight of a crowd of reporters gathered outside the beautiful stone mansion in the middle of the next block.

Sam's house.

"Yeah, Margo, I rely on you to prevent my ego from getting out of control. I'll call you."

"I'll clear my schedule any day for you, sugar. And if you ever decide you want a woman who already knows how to paint…" She hung up, leaving him with a smile on his face.

The smile faded as he wondered how to run this gauntlet of reporters and get to the door, let alone get someone to let him in.

Did he really want to stir up and inflame the reporters like that? Sam would hate it.

A familiar bar-restaurant on the side street between Park and Madison caught his eye, and he turned up the street.

He eased under the yellow awning and greeted the statuesque maître d' with a hug. "Hey, Venetia, the boss here today?"

"He's out on his boat, but I know he'd want me to take care of you. The filet mignon is shockingly good today."

"I've got something a little different in mind. Is there an alley behind this place?"

"Kind of an air shaft." She raised an elegant brow. "Why?"

"Do you have any experience with breaking and entering?"

Sam flashed the mascara wand over her lashes one more time for luck. Sitting at her dressing table, back in her familiar element, she'd managed to calm down considerably.

And embarrassing as it was to admit, she did feel better with her familiar "face" on.

"Ugh. You look disgustingly gorgeous again." Fiona lounged on a chaise in the corner. "I hate you."

A tapping sound on the window made them both turn.

Another familiar face appeared behind the casement. "Louis," they gasped in unison.

Sam darted from her chair. "This is the fourth floor. What the heck?" She yanked open the casement and gripped his arm. "Are you insane?"

"Obviously. If you'll excuse me." With a polite smile, he pulled himself through the opening and climbed down onto the carpet. Followed by a shower of black dirt.

"You need to clean up that wall back there. It's covered with soot from my friend Vincent's kitchen exhaust." Louis's white shirt was filthy, and black smudges disfigured his annoyingly handsome face.

Sam cocked her head and tried to prevent a smile sneaking across her lips. "Then don't you think Vincent should clean it up?"

"I'll leave it to you guys to duke it out." He winked. "So, how's everyone doing?"

"Surprisingly well, under the circumstances." Sam crossed her arms over her chest. Mostly to hide the thickening of her nipples inside her blouse. "But I have no intention of letting the press see you here. How did you know which room it was?"

"I didn't. I've been crawling about on your fire escapes for fifteen minutes."

"And no one saw you?"

"You need better security."

"I guess the staff are all hunkered around the front windows, staring out at the reporters." She squeezed her arms to stop the tingling in her breasts. How could she still be attracted to him even now?

Chemistry, perhaps. Or some other destructive force leading her down the road to ruin.

"You're getting soot on the carpet."

"What kind of nut chooses a white carpet?"

"It's very popular these days. All the chichi designers are installing them." She couldn't fight the smile that snuck over her mouth. "I guess you'd better strip off so we can scrub you clean."

"What a pleasant idea."

Louis reached for the button below his collar.

"I'm out of here." Fiona leaped from the couch with her iPod, and strode for the door.

No one tried to stop her.

Sam narrowed her eyes as the next button revealed an enticing strip of well-toned chest. "That wall has got to be twenty feet high."

"I'd put it closer to thirty." Louis mouth tilted up at one corner. "But it's got quite a few bricks missing."

"Good footholds, huh?"

"Almost like the climbing wall at the gym. You should put some barbed wire on top or something."

He tugged his shirt off and heat flashed through Sam. "I guess I should turn the shower on," she rasped. It was only a few hours since she'd been held by those sturdy arms.

So much had changed since then. Panic flickered through her. "Did any of the reporters see you?"

"I don't think so, but it'll make a good story if they did." He grinned and unbuttoned the fly of his dark pants.

Sam swallowed. "There are helicopters, you know." She could hear vibrating rotors right now.

A knock on the door made them both swing to face it. Louis hesitated, his pants already halfway down his powerful thighs.

Sam dashed forward. "Hold on! Who is it?"

"Mrs. Hardcastle, the security has been breached!" She recognized the high pitched voice of Beatrice, the house-keeper who'd been avoiding her all morning. "The alarms have gone off. There might be an intruder on the premises."

Sam put her hand on the handle to prevent Beatrice from opening it. "I don't hear any alarms." She glanced back at Louis.

Who had the nerve to wink at her as he slid his pants all the way off.

"They're silent."

Sam frowned. "What's the point of that?"

"To alert the staff, of course," said Beatrice, as if talking to an imbecile. "We've summoned the police and they'll be here any moment."

Sam's hand tightened on the handle. "I don't think that's necessary."

For a few, silent seconds, disapproval radiated through the closed oak door. "They're bringing sniffer dogs. They'll search the perimeter and ensure that no one's gained entry. There could be a reporter on the loose inside the house."

Sam could quite picture Beatrice, lips pinched together in disgust at her mistress's blatant disregard for basic safety. Tarrant had thought Beatrice "charmingly old-fashioned." Sam found her to be downright hostile.

She bit her lip. "I suppose it does make sense to check, but please make sure I'm not disturbed." She shot a wide-eyed glance at Louis. "I'm going to…er, take a shower."

"Let me bring some fresh towels. Those ones are from yesterday."

"They're fine, really. It's better for the environment if we use them a few days."

Louis chuckled audibly and Sam shot him a furious glance.

"If you say so, *madam*." The emphasis on the last word was anything but obsequious. "I'll make sure you're not disturbed unless it's absolutely necessary."

"Thank you, Beatrice, I appreciate that." She sank against the door as orthopedic shoes stamped back down the hallway.

She looked up to see Louis, stark naked and breathtakingly gorgeous. "I should throw you to the sniffer dogs."

"I do like dogs." He smiled. "I've never lived in one place long enough to keep one, but I've always wanted to."

"Maybe you should stop traveling so much."

He nodded slowly. "That's what I'm thinking."

She tried to process his words, but her brain didn't seem to be firing on all cylinders.

Hardly surprising with a naked man only feet from her and the house surrounded by reporters and police.

She noticed that he'd rolled up his dirty clothes and placed them carefully on an opened newspaper.

Thoughtful.

Desire unfurled in her belly. "The shower." She walked into

the large bathroom that adjoined her dressing room and turned the giant gold-plated faucets. A reassuring roar of warm water drowned out sound.

Louis followed her into the bathroom. Before she knew what was happening, his lips were over hers and his arms around her back.

She shuddered with a powerful mixture of relief and longing. Nothing felt more natural than being held tight in Louis's arms.

How could that be?

"What are we doing?" she asked, when they finally pulled apart.

"I think they call that kissing."

She blinked. "Your face is still dirty. You'll mess up my makeup."

"Too late." His eyes glittered. "But it's okay because you're coming in the shower with me."

"I just had a shower," she stammered.

"You can't be too clean."

His fingers were already unbuttoning the crisp, striped blouse she'd donned in her attempts to look and feel "respectable."

Why did she care so much about the respect of people who didn't even know her?

Her skin sizzled with awareness as his fingertips brushed her bra. His breath was warm on her neck, quickening along with his obvious arousal.

"What if we're interrupted?" she whispered.

"They won't interrupt you in the shower." He tugged her shirt from her fitted, A-line skirt.

Heat flickered deep inside her. "I suppose you're right."

The room was filling with steam, only some of it generated by the hot water pouring from the six ergonomically designed, gold showerheads.

She heard the *zwick* of her zipper, as Louis's hands moved lower. Her hands wandered of their own accord over his smooth, tanned skin.

A series of loud bangs made Louis freeze. "What was that?"

"It's the water pipes. They're from the 1890s. They get air in them or something. Tarrant always meant to get the house replumbed, but it would mean tearing out the old plaster walls and…hold on, let me stop it before the noise brings Beatrice back."

She leaned into the shower, which splashed her shirt as she turned the faucets off for a second.

In the momentary silence, she heard the wail of a police siren. Fear crowded her brain. "We can't do this."

"What, take a shower?" Louis's voice was muffled by her breasts. He'd crouched to lower her skirt and had somehow gotten distracted.

"No, *this*, anything! Are we insane? The house is surrounded by armed police and aggressive reporters who'll do anything for a story."

"You shouldn't let yourself get distracted by things you can't control." His lips brushed her belly button, making her insides flutter.

Desperation welled inside her. "I don't feel like I can control anything. Even my own body. Although my brain is screaming at me to take cover, all I want to do is get in that shower and…and…"

Make love with you.

Even in her feverish state, she didn't say the words. There had been no talk of *love* between them.

Louis rose and placed his hands on her waist. "Didn't you receive some advice to follow your heart?"

Sam frowned. "Madame Ayida? Oh, please, I'm sure she just makes that stuff up to entertain the tourists. What kind of a cliché is 'follow your heart,' anyway?"

"A powerful one." He buried his face in her neck and pressed his lips softly to her skin. "I followed mine here."

His deep voice penetrated her fog of anxiety. "Your heart?"

He looked up, and met her gaze with those haunting eyes. "I do have one, you know, despite what they say."

"And what is it telling you?" She spoke slowly, her voice shaking. Maybe he'd say something that would let them both off the hook.

That would be fine. Good even.

Her heart hammered behind her ribs.

"It's telling me I've met a very special woman. A woman so generous and caring that people assume she must have an ulterior motive."

Frowning, he looked into her eyes. "A woman who has so much love to give that the world can't seem to absorb it all and keeps throwing it back in her face."

He brushed her cheek with his thumb. "And I'm not fool enough to let you throw away what we've found together."

Sam's heart squeezed. She managed to keep her breathing under control. "What have we found?"

She cursed herself instantly after asking the stupid question. What did she want to hear? That he loved her?

How lame could she get? She didn't even want him to love her. They couldn't have any kind of relationship given the weird family situation, so the whole thing was just pointless and stupid and painful and…

A whimper escaped her mouth as Louis took her into his

embrace and held her so tight she couldn't possibly escape even if she wanted to.

Which she didn't.

In a swift motion he lifted her into the shower and kissed her hard as warm water cascaded over them.

"I'm still wearing my underwear," she protested, when he let her up for air.

"Not for long," he growled. He unfastened her bra with a deft movement of his fingers, and tugged her soaked panties down over her legs.

He rose, dripping. "Much better." His voice was hoarse with the longing that echoed between them. Louis's hands roamed over her body, smearing the water over her skin until she moaned and writhed under his touch.

His arousal had gathered into a hard arrow of need, pointing right at her. She took him in her hand, and he released a low groan.

"I want you inside me," she murmured, hardly able to believe she was saying it aloud. "Now."

Louis replied with his body, entering her with swift passion that made her gasp with pleasure.

He hadn't answered her question about what they'd found. He didn't need to. They'd found…this. Physical closeness, of a raw, intense and human kind that she'd never experienced before. It added a dimension to their emotional connection that made her feel…whole.

They writhed and twisted under the steady flow of water. She let her hands wander over the masculine curves of his body, into his damp hair.

Louis kissed her face and neck and held her steady in his arms as she let wave after wave of vicious pleasure wash over her.

It took her a moment to realize Louis was saying something. His voice blended with the roar of the water and the roar of sensation and emotion inside her, but his words snuck through the curtain of bliss and she realized he was trying to answer her question.

"We've found…" His words were guttural, filled with emotion. "We've found…" he repeated and then he hesitated, still moving inside her, talking to her with his body.

Then he stopped.

The interruption was jarring, and she opened her eyes. Louis stared at her, water cascading over his striking face.

"Sam, will you marry me?"

Nine

Sam disentangled herself from Louis and flew out of the shower, half skidded on the marble floor and grabbed a towel before fleeing into the bedroom.

Had he really asked what she thought he had asked?

No. It wasn't possible. Her mind was playing tricks on her.

Her heart thundered and her brain raced like a roller coaster.

"Sam." Louis appeared in the steamy doorway, a towel wrapped around his middle. "That wasn't quite the response I was hoping for."

"I'm sorry. I had to get out. I thought I… I thought you…" She didn't know what she thought. Mostly she just wanted to get away from Louis and the alarming pull he seemed to have on her.

Louis moved up behind her, still dripping. She held herself steady and tried not to shiver as he buried his face in her wet hair. "Will you?"

Sam gulped. "Will I what?"

"Marry me."

He said it simply, with no roguish charm or humor.

Like he really and truly meant it.

Sam wheeled to face him. "You can't be serious."

"I've never been more serious in my life."

Sam's chest tightened. She stepped away from him. "There's a lot more to a marriage than great sex. Trust me, I've been married three times and there wasn't great sex in any of them."

"Maybe that's part of the problem." She could hear humor in his husky voice.

She recoiled from him. "It doesn't matter anyway, because I'm done being married." Her voice rose, trembling with emotion. "Three times is enough for one lifetime. I'll always cherish the memories of my time with Tarrant, but I'm not going to ever marry again."

"You don't mean that."

Sam wheeled around, heart pounding. "Don't tell me what I mean! I don't need a father and I don't need a big brother, either. I've lived and learned a lot of things the hard way and I can make up my own mind, whether you like it or not."

She stormed out of the room and slammed the door behind her. Too late she realized she'd just slammed herself into her walk-in closet.

Hopefully Louis would have the decency to *go away*. Preferably the way he came, so no one would see him.

Her breath came in ragged gasps. Marry him? Was this some kind of cruel joke at her expense?

All she wanted was to be left alone.

"Sam." His low voice filtered through the wooden slats. "You're in a closet."

"I know," she half shouted, so angry at him she wanted to scream. Who was he to play with her emotions? She was fragile before she met him and now—

A half sob caught in her throat.

"Let me in."

"No!"

"Then I'll huff, and I'll puff and I'll—"

"Louis, it's not funny," she panted. "Please, just leave me in peace. I need to be alone."

"No, you don't. You've spent way too much time alone and you need to be with me."

"Ha," was all she could manage to say, as his words rattled around in her poor overtaxed brain.

Then a welcome retort found its way to her lips. "You're crazy. You read that article. I'm *The Merry Widow,* remember? The *gold-digging tramp* who married Tarrant for his money."

She fisted her hands into a red crushed-velvet dress. "Everywhere I go, there's some maniac with a camera hoping to capture a picture of me in a compromising position so they can make money from my miserable existence." She tugged at the dress so hard that it popped off the hanger. "No one wants to be a part of that. No one should be a part of that." Her voice ended in a whimper.

She saw the knob turn and couldn't summon the strength to stop it. Louis eased into the dim space of the closet and closed the door behind him.

It was pretty big, as closets go, but there was still less than two feet of space between them. His freshly clean, male scent tickled her nostrils. Drops of water glistened on his skin and hung from his damp hair.

"You came after me, remember? I was just going about my own business."

Sam bit her lip. "Maybe it was a mistake."

"You opened Pandora's box." His eyes glittered in the half-light sneaking in through a crack in the door.

"The Greek myth where a woman gets curious and unleashes evils on the world?" She clutched her towel closer.

He did blame her.

"Yes, slander, greed, vanity, envy, falsehood, scandal…" He cocked his head. "Those things do seem to be loose in our world right now."

She avoided his glance. "I should have left you alone."

"No." He seized her hand. Her fingers trembled inside his hot grasp. "There was one more thing in the box, the most important one, that didn't escape. She didn't let it." His eyes met hers. "Hope."

Something flashed between them as he held her gaze and mouthed the word, so soft she could barely hear it.

"Hope," she repeated, unable to stop herself.

"You awakened something in me, Sam, something that wasn't there before." A flicker of confusion crossed his brow. "I always thought I knew what I wanted in life, and that I had it, too. But since I met you, I know I want more." He squeezed her hand. "I *need* more."

Her heart constricted, as if he held it in his hand, too. "I'm sure you'll find it." Her voice sounded thin. "With some nice girl who doesn't have a cartload of baggage and a crowd of vultures circling around her head."

"I don't want a nice girl." He edged closer to her. The closet was getting hot, water drops on their skin almost evaporating into steam. "I want a woman. One who isn't afraid to make the life she wants. That's you, Sam. You've been brave enough to start over again and again, and you're not done yet."

She looked past him into the gloom, where her much photographed outfits, each one laced with memory, hung in regular rows. "I'm not done with life, but I'm all done with marriage. Three is enough."

"Says who? Zsa Zsa would disagree. And you two have a fair amount in common if this wardrobe is anything to go by." He fingered a bold-patterned Gautier gown.

Sam lifted her chin. "You're very argumentative."

"It's part of my charm."

His hands wandered through her clothes, plundering them, his fingers roaming through the luxurious fabrics just as they'd roved over her skin. Which tingled with...annoyance. "Why are you in my closet?"

He hesitated, his eyes wandering to her mouth, which twitched, and her throat, which gulped, before replying, "because you're here." Louis lifted his hand and cupped her cheek. "I love you, Sam."

The words closed around her heart like a fist, then swept away on a wave of panic. "You can't."

"I don't take orders well." His golden eyes glinted a challenge.

"Everything's too complicated."

"Nothing complicated about love." He brushed a drop of water from her lip with his thumb. "Do you love me, Sam?"

She froze. *Yes* screamed across her brain. "No."

He cocked his head. "I don't believe you."

"You're shockingly arrogant, you know that?" Her voice rose.

"Yes." A smile flickered across his lips. "I know what I want and I'm not afraid to go after it."

"Maybe you should think about someone else for a change." Her hands shook. "I have responsibilities to this family and to the whole Hardcastle corporation."

His eyes narrowed. "And to yourself."

"Exactly." Sam shoved a hand through her tangled hair. "I'm thirty-one and I've been through three husbands. There's something wrong with that picture, don't you think?"

"I don't think there's anything wrong with it at all." He held her gaze. "It's unique. It's your journey and you're a beautiful person."

Beautiful?

Sam cringed at the thought of what she must look like right now. Lucky she couldn't see herself. Louis of course looked breathtaking. The shaft of light through the closet door sculpted his torso in gold, while water dripped erotically from his shiny, dark curls.

"What is going through that intriguing mind of yours?"

She tilted her head. "Just mulling some artistic options."

A smile slid across his lips. "As you should be. You've a lot to accomplish, Sam, and some lost time to make up for."

"As it happens, I agree with you there. I've decided that I will take up painting. And I won't even be mad at myself if I stink at it."

"That's the attitude. I knew you'd see it my way eventually. Now, back to my other question."

Sam shrank into her towel. "I can't marry you. It's preposterous that you even thought of it. Even if you weren't my *stepson*." She shuddered involuntarily. "We barely know each other."

"We have a deeper connection than most people."

She narrowed her eyes. "Is this some New Orleans voodoo psychic angle you're working here? I'm not as gullible as I look."

"Remember what Madame Ayida said?"

"Follow my heart. Yeah, sure. I'm not even sure there's one

in there after all this time." She glanced mockingly down to where her hands crossed over her towel. "Don't forget she also mentioned the two roads, neither of which seemed to lead anywhere I'd want to go."

Louis looked at her for a second, then laughed. "How do you know if you haven't walked on one yet? Didn't she say one is familiar and one is strange?"

Sam crossed her arms over her chest, which left her fumbling for her towel. "If you look at it that way, then it's getting married that's familiar, and not getting married that would be strange. I'll go with strange."

"Fine. We can live in sin."

She couldn't help laughing at his deadpan comeback.

Then her smile faded. "I'm sure the tabloid press would enjoy that."

"Absolutely. We'll really help 'em sell some copies. Just think, if we have a bunch of kids, they could accuse you of being mother to your own grandchildren." His eyes shone with humor.

Sam froze. *Children.* She'd told him how much she wanted a child, so his comment was a low blow.

"Tarrant's children are my children," she said stiffly.

"Including me, I guess."

"Yes." She gave him the hardest stare she could muster. "That's my preference."

"You can't have kids your own age."

"Sure you can."

They stared at each other.

He blinked first.

"You think *I'm* stubborn," he said, eyes glinting. "You're downright delusional."

"Then leave me alone with my delusions. We're happy together."

Louis stared at her for a moment, then laughed, slowly. "You've certainly got the wardrobe to be a delusional billionaire widow." Then his eyes narrowed. "But I won't let you throw your life away."

He leaned in until his words vibrated off her skin. "You're meant to be a mother, and not some kind of fake, fairy-godmother type of mother, but a real mother who has to get up in the night because her baby is crying, and has to miss an important meeting because her toddler has a fever and has to relearn long division to help her nine-year-old with his homework."

A flash of pain almost blinded her. How would he know that she craved the challenges of parenthood as much as the photo-album moments people raved about?

She tried to keep her breathing steady. "I thought you didn't want kids."

"I didn't know what the heck I wanted until I met you, Sam." Emotion darkened in his voice and shone in his eyes.

Her insides churned and she felt her grip on reality growing more fragile.

"This is insanity. Why are we standing here with no clothes on?"

"I don't have any clean clothes." He looked at her, eyes glinting. "And I don't think yours would suit me."

Sam blinked. Swallowed. "Some of Tarrant's are still in the other closet." She pointed to the door. The air was so thick she could barely breathe. "Help yourself."

She collapsed against the rack of clothes as he opened the door and slipped out.

Her heart rattled like a runaway train.

Why did the craziest things seem possible with him around?

Get dressed. She didn't want to be standing around in a

towel when the police came to the door with their sniffer dogs searching for an intruder.

Especially since she was harboring one.

The racks of couture originals usually comforted her, the rich colors and fabrics a balm to her spirit. Today they seemed to hang around her like carcasses.

I bet you'd look cute in a pair of Levi's.

Louis crept into her consciousness. Of course there weren't any Levi's to be found. There was one pair of Circle of Seven jeans folded up on the top shelf. A gift from Fiona that she'd never found occasion to wear.

Sam pulled them down and climbed into them. She tugged on a fitted black shirt and buttoned it, fingers shaking. Maybe she could just stay in the closet all day and not go out to face the mess that she'd made of her life.

Or Louis.

"Are you still in there, or is there a secret tunnel to Barneys?" His voice resounded through the wood door.

Sam smiled. "I wish there was a secret tunnel."

She braced herself as the door opened. He stood there in a pair of pale linen pants and a loose shirt. She couldn't recall ever having seen Tarrant in that outfit, which was no surprise since he'd had almost as many clothes as she did. "You look nice," she stammered, to cover the awkwardness she felt.

"I am nice."

"I'm not so sure about that."

"I want to spend the rest of my life proving it to you."

He reached for her hand, but Sam shrank back. "Be sensible. They're looking for an intruder, remember?" Suddenly her mind was clear and clicking. In crisis mode. "We've got to get you out of here somehow. Now, how can we do it without the staff seeing you?" She pressed a hand to her temple. "Maybe we can get you down to the underground garage and into the car with the tinted—"

A high-pitched noise made her jump. "My phone."

She ran forward and snatched it off the dressing table.

"Where the hell have you been?" cried Fiona, the moment she pressed it to her ear. "I was pounding on the door. I figured maybe you went out on the fire escape or something. What's going on?"

Sam gulped. "We… I…" She didn't dare look up at Louis.

"On second thought, I don't want to know. I've been trying to find you because Dominic and Amado are here."

Sam's heart stopped.

"They're out in the street arguing with the reporters. Turn on your TV to Channel Five. Or heck, just open a window."

Sam ran past Louis, grabbed the remote from her dressing table and flicked on the TV above Tarrant's dressing table on the opposite wall. It reflected into her mirror right next to her own startled expression.

In a surreal montage, her own front door floated above her cosmetics bottles, decorated with a familiar network logo. Dominic stood on the steps, his proud features rigid. "This rumor is ridiculous, and neither Hardcastle Enterprises nor the Hardcastle family will take it lying down."

His face loomed as he neared the camera lens. "If you don't retract this ludicrous story about my stepmother, Samantha, having an affair with my brother Louis, we'll sue you for libel." His lips settled into a hard line.

The reporters exploded into a blur of sound and motion. Sam staggered back, heart pounding. "Oh, no. We've got to stop them…" she murmured into the phone. "How can we get him inside?"

Just then an incensed Amado took a swing at a reporter who'd shoved a microphone in his face.

Worry propelled her out of the room, phone still pressed to her ear. "Beatrice, open the front door!" she shouted down the wide stairs as she shoved out into the hallway.

"We can't. The mob will break in."

"Dominic and Amado are out there. They could be hurt." She ran down the stairs, bare feet cool on the limestone.

If no one else around here was brave enough to open the door, she'd do it herself.

"Madame, don't go out there!" Beatrice and Sam's assistant Kelly mobbed her in the front hall.

She pushed past them, single-minded, tugged on the heavy brass locks and yanked the door open, then blinked as light flooded in from the street outside. "Dom, Amado!"

She couldn't even make them out in the throng of bodies. Microphones and cameras thrust toward her. Voices and clatter and commotion rose into a roar of sound that assaulted her ears. *Is it true? Are you having an affair? What about the photographic evidence?*

The clamor assaulted her ears and she shrank back. "Dominic, Amado, where are you?"

Dominic's dark head thrust through the crowd. "Sam, thank God you've come out to defend yourself. I won't let them treat you like this. Tell them it's a lie."

Sam's mouth opened, but no words came out.

To tell that it's a lie would be...a lie.

"Come here, Sam." Dominic stood right in front of her on the top step now, his face dark with anger. "Tell these vultures that you won't put up with their bull anymore."

"I...I...I..."

Amado pushed through the crowd, looking disheveled and

irate. "This is a crime. An assault on an innocent woman in her own home. These people should be behind bars."

Dom and Amado flanked her, and she felt their strong hands holding her up. "Go on, Sam, tell them."

Silence throbbed as the gathered throng waited for her reply. Even the birds seemed to stop singing, and the traffic on Park Avenue ground to a halt.

"Come on, Sam, defend yourself," murmured Dominic.

She hesitated, blood pounding in her brain. "I…I…I can't."

She turned and plunged back into the house. She heard Dominic and Amado, pressing the reporters back. They both managed to get through the door and closed it behind them.

All of them stood, panting, in the hallway for a split second.

Then Dominic moved forward and put his hands on her shoulders. "Sam, what do you mean?" She shivered under his forceful touch.

Her voice wouldn't come out. She dragged in a shaky breath. "I can't deny it."

"Why not?" His dark eyes peered into hers.

"Because it's true."

Shock washed over Dominic's face. "It can't be."

He pulled his hands from her shoulders, a move so sudden it made her flinch.

Confusion contorted Amado's handsome features. "What do you mean, Sam?"

The entire household staff gathered in the hallway; Beatrice and Kelly, the cook and her assistant, even Raul the ancient repairman who'd been with the house since its previous owner. Fiona stood behind him, her iPod unplugged from her ears and her face pale.

All hung on her reply.

"Louis and I have…have…" She cursed herself for being unable to form a whole sentence.

But what was a polite—or even halfway decent—way to tell them what had really happened?

"We're in love." A deep voice resonated along the marble hallway.

Sam looked up and saw Louis at the top of the stairs.

Something hot and unfamiliar swelled inside her.

She crushed it down, angry that he'd made a public declaration even though she'd made it clear she couldn't marry him. Some things weren't meant to be.

Dominic and Amado stared at each other, then back at Sam.

"I'm so sorry," she whispered to them. They were both so traditional, so worried about honor and the family reputation. They made her feel safe and protected.

And she'd betrayed them.

"Is it true?" Amado took her hand.

"I…" What exactly was he asking? Was it true that she was in love with Louis?

Panic surged through her. She was recently widowed and still grieving her dead husband, she had no idea what she felt about anything.

"It started by accident," she stammered. "When we first met I had no idea who he was, and I tried to stop, but—" The words jammed in her throat.

"But we couldn't." Louis materialized beside her, tall and self-assured.

He shrugged, maybe a hint of apology in his expression as he looked at Dominic and Amado. "We should have told you earlier, so you didn't waste your energy arguing with the rabble out there."

His casual "we" stirred a warmth, mingled with fury at the

way he spoke so easily for both of them. Couldn't she even express her own thoughts without someone jumping in to put words in her mouth?

She glanced at Dominic. His face would make quite a painting. A baroque mask of horror somewhere between Goya and El Greco.

Her stomach curled into a knot.

Then he started to laugh. The sound boomed through the wide marble entrance hall and up the stairs. Contagious, it rippled first to Amado, then Fiona, then to the junior staffers.

Louis joined in, then even Sam found herself unable to control the explosive release of tension.

"They are going to *love* this."

"It really isn't funny," gasped Sam. Horrible, breathy bursts of laughter exploded from her throat. Hysteria. Everything was moving too fast, going all wrong.

"It is, though," Dominic's often serious face bore a huge grin. "And it's wonderful. I thought you had a mysterious glow ever since you came back from New Orleans. I figured it was because you were so excited to find Louis, now I can see it was a little more than that."

Sam wrung her hands. "I didn't want anyone to find out."

"Why? You're not related," said Amado. "It's a family tradition to fall madly in love with the wrong person. Look at Dominic, getting involved with a corporate spy planning to sue his father, and me, crazy about the woman who showed up to destroy my family." He grinned. "Welcome to the club, Louis."

Louis, standing calm and unruffled, smiled and glanced at Sam. "You okay?"

"I have no idea," she said honestly. She suspected not. There was an unpleasant pulsing sensation in her left temple and her heart kept beating faster. "What about Tarrant?"

Fiona stepped forwards. "He's probably laughing his head off somewhere. You know he wanted you to live a full life after he died."

Sam wrapped her arms around herself as grief cascaded through her, cold and painful. "He said that, but I know he didn't really mean it. I promised him that he'd be the last." She tried to keep her breathing steady, to remain standing as her legs grew shaky.

"And he told me to make sure he wasn't." Fiona winked. "If I know my dad, he'd be on the phone trying to hook up an exclusive deal to sell the story for a million bucks." She glanced at Dominic.

"Don't look at me." Dominic narrowed his eyes. "I took over his role in the company, but I didn't turn into him."

Fiona bit her lip. "What about Sam's charities? We could sell the story to raise money for Save the Children or something."

"Hey, that's not a bad idea." Louis half smiled.

Sam's ears rang with all these lunatic suggestions. The hallway had started to pulse and throb with color. The floor had grown wobbly and unsteady under her and she wasn't sure she could keep standing much longer.

Her train was going off the tracks.

"You're standing here talking about my personal life like I don't even exist." Her high-pitched wail rang through the hallway.

She gasped for air, a sob rising dangerously in her throat. She stared right at Louis. "I'm a grown-up. I can make up my own mind. I don't need anyone to tell me what to do." Even as she tried to convince them that she was rational, her mind seemed to be shattering, thoughts and sensations clashing and colliding into a kaleidoscopic nightmare.

She needed to get away. "Please, don't follow me."

As tears clouded her eyes, she ran for the stairs.

"Sam." Louis's voice vaguely penetrated the roar of blood in her ears as a wave of hurt and anger crashed over her. Now she was crying in front of Dom and Amado and Fiona and all the staff. She'd wanted so badly to be a reassuring mother figure to them all, nurturing them and supporting them, instead she was a hysterical wreck. A source of scandal and humiliation.

She flew up five flights of stairs, right to the top of the house. She paused for breath, hands gripping the polished baluster.

No one followed. Good. At least they had some sense of decency not to hound her in the supposed privacy of her own home.

She unlatched the door to the roof deck, flung it open and plunged outside into the bright sunlight. The sky crouched over her, bright and clear. She gulped air, trying to stop the horrible sobbing sounds racking her body and escaping through her trembling lips.

One minute everything was okay. Fine. Wonderful even. The next minute the world was crashing in. She didn't seem to have any control over her own body, or even her own thoughts. *She couldn't live like this.*

She wouldn't live like this.

If she continued on this course, the tabloids were quite capable of hounding them for years, of disrupting all their lives and damaging the company's reputation.

It hadn't been easy to transform herself into Samantha Hardcastle, wife of one of the most powerful men in the world. She'd achieved considerable success, raising money for charities, cultivating friendships with people who were important to the company, helping to promote Hardcastle Enterprises and enhance its reputation in everything she did.

And most importantly, she'd worked hard to build the Hardcastle family and sustain it now that Tarrant was gone.

Her selfish, personal desires could not be allowed to draw hostile attention and ugly innuendo to her private circle.

Sam dragged in a long, shuddering breath of air. Her pulse rate slowed and the jagged edge of tears started to subside.

Good.

She'd made her decision, and this time she was sticking with it.

Louis pushed open the door to the roof. Sunlight blinded him and he raised a hand to shield his eyes. Sam stood, a frail figure in her skinny jeans and dark shirt, silhouetted against the bright sky.

Of course she was upset. He understood. Once he held her, she'd...

"It's over between us." She hurled the words at him like a handful of stones.

"Relax, Sam. You're just upset because of the press."

She held his gaze, her blue eyes bright. "I'm not upset, or overwrought or hysterical. I'm perfectly rational, and I've made the right decision."

Irritation rippled through him. "For who?"

"For *me*. And despite what you and all the other men in my past might think, I'm quite capable of making decisions for myself." She crossed her hands over her chest, defensive. "Or do you disagree?"

She'd issued a challenge. If he did disagree, he was no better than the other men in her life who'd tried to tell her what to do.

He spoke softly. "I think you should take some time to reflect. We could go to Europe for a while, Barcelona, perhaps. I have business to do there and we could..."

Sam squeezed her eyes shut. "No! I'm not running away.

I don't want to go to Europe or anywhere else. I just want to stop this crazy affair that's going to derail all of our lives if we let it."

How could he make her see without proving that he didn't respect her? For once words seemed to have deserted him, so he simply took a step toward her.

"Stop! Don't push me, Louis. I've made up my mind and all I ask is that you respect my decision."

Her delicate features now formed a mask of determination that echoed in her stern voice.

She was shutting him out and bolting the door.

A wave of desperation unleashed a tide of anger. "There are two of us in this relationship." His voice emerged as a growl.

"No. There is no relationship." Her expression didn't alter. She'd morphed into the polished society matron smiling from the party pages in the magazines. "It's all over. Now I'd appreciate you leaving me in peace."

He stared at her, his mind reeling. *He'd offered her his heart…his whole life.*

He planned to raise a family with her, something he'd never imagined doing, but that he now wanted with a painful and unfamiliar urgency.

He'd offered her *everything he had,* and now she replied with a haughty dismissal.

A steel band of emotion tightened around his chest and his muscles ached and throbbed.

But he wasn't going to beg.

Without another word, he turned and strode for the door.

Ten

"Samantha, darling, you've outdone yourself! Everyone—simply everyone—has been talking about this party for days. Who did the flowers? Marcel? He's such a talent, such an artist…"

Sam kept her smile in place while Cecilia Dawson-Crane exclaimed over the lilies. She should be glad. She put a lot of effort into getting those damn lilies just right.

So why did she feel like such a fraud standing here? The grand ballroom was abuzz with chat and laughter. She was surrounded by two thousand of her closest friends, all of whom had paid hundreds of dollars for the privilege of joining her for an intimate gourmet dinner.

She'd already raised over a million dollars, not including the raffle, for the World Refugee Fund. She should be ecstatic.

Instead she felt…desperate.

"Samantha, sweetheart!" She swung around to kiss another powdered cheek, this one belonging to her friend, Kitty. "Congratulations on snagging an art show."

Sam blushed. "It's just the church hall."

"It's not any old church hall, it's on Madison Avenue and I'm bringing all my art world friends."

"You're sweet. I just started experimenting with oils and I'm not sure I'm ready, but Margo insisted. And if anyone's foolish enough to buy one, it'll help pay for the church's new roof."

"Everyone will want one. Mark my words. I'm not the number-one selling agent for Darcy and Maclaine for no reason. Who knew you had so much talent hidden under that well-sculpted exterior?"

Not me, that's for sure. A few lessons with Louis's friend Margo had unlocked something inside Sam that had her up in her new studio day and night, diving into a turpentine-scented world of light and color.

"I do enjoy painting so much."

"Trust me, we can tell by looking at your work. That big one of the Louisiana bayou at dusk..." Kitty shook her head, which had no effect whatsoever on her spiky blond tresses. "It's magic."

Sam gulped. She'd been reluctant to include that in the show, given all the potboiler publicity over her affair with Louis. But Margo insisted that was all forgotten. And she was pretty much right. Since Sam never responded to the accusations and Louis had left for Europe, people assumed it was just more lies.

So she'd agreed to include the painting of Louis's special place. "That was my first painting."

"You're kidding?" Kitty's hazel eyes widened.

"No, it formed in my mind one morning and I couldn't put down the brush until it was done. It took me three days and nights. Anna brought me meals in my studio." She touched Kitty's forearm. "Lucky thing I'm a lady of leisure, huh?"

Kitty stared. "First of all, I've never met anyone in my life who works harder than you. Second of all…wow. I'm going to be keeping an eye on you as an investment, as well as a friend."

Sam flushed with pride. It seemed she actually was good at painting. Louis had been right about that.

Ugh, why did he keep sneaking into her mind when she least expected? Even painting and lunching and making phone calls around the clock didn't squeeze him out of her consciousness.

Especially at night. When she was in bed. Alone.

She excused herself from Kitty and hurried to the green room to see how the speakers were doing, then checked with the caterers on whether the take-home gifts were ready.

Everything in place. All going smoothly.

"Sam-mee!"

Sam tried not to roll her eyes at the annoying name only one person called her. "Hi, Bethanne," she said and kissed her on both cheeks. "How's the house in Amagansett coming?"

"Appallingly slow, but what do you expect? Apparently the marble shipment from Italy got impounded by customs or some such nonsense. But never mind that, where are those dangerously handsome young men you rounded up to be your lifelong consorts?"

Sam blinked. "Oh, you mean Dominic and Amado and…" Her throat closed as she tried to say Louis's name.

"Of course I do. What a marvelous idea to have sturdy young knights at your disposal and you don't even have to sleep with them. Honestly, some aspects of marriage are better left unexplored after a certain age." She winked a heavily mascaraed eyelash. "I don't imagine you'll remarry, dear, will you? Too much trouble defending your fortune from young turks, what with prenups being overturned in the courts every day. No, I wouldn't, either, in your shoes."

Bethanne Demarist leaned in, until her horrid scent threatened to choke Sam, "But just between you and me, I could quite understand enjoying the talents of those adorable young men."

"Dominic and Amado are both married," stammered Sam.

"That's not who I was talking about," replied Bethanne, with a knowing look.

"I...I...I must see if the hors d'oeuvres are being circulated."

"Come on, Sammy. I saw that picture in the paper."

"We weren't kissing. It was a trick of the light."

Bethanne narrowed her eyes. "A trick of the light, huh?"

"Yes, and you'd be amazed what they can do with digital photography these days." *And how easily I can tell a bold-faced fib on this topic.*

She really should be ashamed to outright lie about it. But it was in self-defense. And people got off even for murder when it was in self-defense, right?

"Ah, well," Bethanne's expression slipped into a smirk. "I have seen him pictured with a lot of beautiful women since then."

Sam blanched. She had, too. Over the winter he'd opened another restaurant, come second in a prestigious yacht race and judged a big film festival. The pictures of Louis entwined with a succession of gorgeous starlet types had tied her stomach in knots for days on end.

Which was ridiculous. She should be glad to see him enjoying himself.

"Exactly," Sam stammered. "He's got a busy life. That's why he's not here tonight."

"Trick of the light. I'll have to remember that one." With a wink, Bethanne melted into the crowd.

Sometimes she could barely remember the feel of his hands on her skin. Then, all at once, her skin would hum with sensation and she'd feel like he was right there.

Which he wasn't. *Trick of the senses.*

Everything in her life was going better than she could have dreamed. She'd visited Argentina for Christmas and Amado and Susannah had shared that they were expecting their first child. She'd already spent many happy hours fondling toy catalogs and she was secretly making a quilt.

Dominic had taken the retail sector of Hardcastle Enterprises to a whole new level by combining it with his own chain of stores, and his genius wife, Bella, had come up with a revolutionary sunblock that protected the skin from harmful rays, but allowed valuable vitamin D production.

She should be over the moon to be part of—even a catalyst behind—all the wonderful things going on around her.

Instead she felt hollow and empty inside. Even the joy of creating new worlds on canvas didn't fill the hole that seemed to gape a little wider each day.

She missed Louis.

Maybe she should just call to say hi. This long silence between them was awkward. Unsettling. It undermined everything she'd hoped for about drawing the Hardcastle family
closer.

They could chat and everything would be more…normal.
Right?

"Wrong." Sam's heart sank as she looked up at Fiona.
They sat curled up on the sofa in the Plum Room at the
mansion. "The number, that is. Not in service."

"Maybe Louis got a new cell?"

"Could be. I tried the house first, and I keep getting the
machine. I don't want to leave a message. You never know
who could hear it and start trouble. He must have staff coming
in and out since he's out of town so much."

"You're just going to have to go down there and find him."
Fiona scrolled through her iPod playlist, as if she could care
less either way.

"How would I even know if he's in town?"

"He's in town." Fiona grabbed her PDA off the floor,
pressed a few keys and handed it to Sam. "Party at his restaurant in the Quarter last night. Big jazz honchos all there."

Sam peered at the image on the tiny screen. Sure enough,
there on a Web site called "Glitterati" was Louis, surrounded
by smiling people she didn't recognize.

Her pulse picked up. So, he was down in New Orleans,
right now.

"You could be at LaGuardia in forty-five minutes," murmured Fiona without looking up.

"Mmm-hmm." Sam bit her lip. "I really should go, don't
you think? For the good of the family?"

A sly smile crept around Fiona's mouth. "Absolutely."

* * *

A light mist of rain fell through the dark as Sam rang Louis's doorbell. Her heart thudded and her palms were damp, but a sense of resolve and determination straightened her back. She had nothing to be ashamed of. She was human, and so was Louis. Life was short and meant to be lived.

And she wanted to live hers with Louis.

A light shone from the back of the house, and she could imagine Louis sitting upstairs in his office, or maybe eating a late dinner in the elegant dining room she could imagine, overlooking a garden.

She peered through the small squares of glass behind the scrolled wrought iron on the door, and saw a shadowy figure moving along the hallway. The door swung open to reveal an elegant older woman with her hair swept up into a white bun on top of her head.

"Yes?" The woman looked her up and down, which made Sam self-conscious. Her dress was wrinkled from travel and already damp from the rain.

"Is Louis here?" Sam tried to stop her voice from shaking.

"He's not expected back until morning." The woman raised a brow. "Can I take a message?" She had an air of wariness, like she's spent all night taking messages from forlorn women.

Which maybe she had.

"Um, do you know where he is?"

The woman's lips pursed. "I'm not at liberty to say."

Gone until morning. Which meant he was staying the night somewhere else. And why would he do that if there wasn't a woman involved?

Sam's heart clenched like a fist. She'd come too late. She'd seen those pictures of him with other women, but somewhere, deep inside, she'd assumed they were just pictures. Standing there, with rain dripping off the balcony behind her, she realized that all along she'd imagined Louis waiting patiently for her to come to her senses.

But now that she had, he was gone.

"Could you tell me the address of his fishing cabin? I'd like to visit it again before I go and I can't remember the way." Her lip quivered. At least of she was going back to New York alone she could get one more look at the bayou that had inspired her to start painting.

But the woman crossed her arms over her ample chest. "I'm afraid that address is strictly private. Would you like to leave a message for Mr. DuLac?"

Clearly she wanted to sweep Sam off her doorstep and get back to her quiet evening inside. But what message could Sam leave? It would only be awkward if Louis knew she'd come looking for him and had learned he was out all night with another woman.

"No message, thanks. Sorry to bother you."

"No problem, good night." With a forced smile, the woman closed the door, leaving Sam alone in the damp, dark street. She let out a shuddering sigh as disappointment soaked through her like rain.

As she wrapped her fingers around the handle of her rental car, ready to head back to the airport, she resolved to at least drive to the bayou to say goodbye. Even if she couldn't find the spot where Louis lived, she could sit there for a while and listen to the rain. Maybe even wait for the sunrise. If nothing else, another painting might come to her. The ability to create a private place and make it come alive on canvas was a surprising comfort in an unpredictable world, and her world was nothing if not unpredictable.

* * *

Louis swerved to avoid a large box turtle on the road. The tires skidded a little on the rain-soaked asphalt and he struggled to stay on the pavement.

Damn! Katie said she'd left hours ago. She hadn't even intended for him to find out she'd come. But when Katie described a tall, skinny woman with big blue eyes in a crazy-looking dress and high heels, he could only picture one person.

In all likelihood, Sam was on a plane back to New York right now, but instinct drove him deeper into the bayou country. Katie said she'd asked for the address of his cabin. Fiona had told him about the painting Sam did—the swamp afire with light—and that everyone was raving about her talent and begging for more of the same. Would she seek the scene of her inspiration in hope of finding more?

Maybe that was why she'd come down here in the first place.

He shouldn't delude himself that she'd come down here looking for *him*. Lord knew he'd done his best to get her out of his mind, opening the new café in Nice, keeping busy with friends.

With women.

A thick rope of sensation tugged at his chest. Nothing had helped. He only wanted one woman, and she'd shoved him out of her life like yesterday's garbage.

As a member of New York's high society she must be used to doing that. Probably changed her friends as often as she updated her expensive wardrobe.

Louis stuck his arm out the window of the car into the mist of rain hovering over the bayou. The drops felt cool and peaceful on his sweaty skin.

He'd told himself he'd get over her.

Eventually.

But so far it hadn't happened, and if tonight's high-speed chase along rain-streaked bayou roads was anything to go by, he was a long, long way from over her.

He turned onto the side road that led to the cabin just as the first silvery streaks of dawn rose above the swamp. For some reason he already felt closer to her. Which was ridiculous. There was nothing for miles but swaying grass and overgrown trees on a blue-gray haze of rain.

But he'd never really managed to banish memories of her bright smile, her hopeful gaze, the warmth that emanated from her like the steam rising from his car engine.

Even now, longing crept through his muscles and made his nerves kick with desire.

He pulled up by the boathouse. Was that a gleam of something in the dark? He jumped out of the car and strode toward the wood structure that stood silent and invisible in the damp darkness. Rain soaked through his shirt and cooled his skin, but it didn't ease the dull ache in his chest. The constant sense of yearning for the one thing he wanted and couldn't have.

"Sam."

His voice echoed around the empty swamp. He must be delusional to come here looking for her. Still, as he walked around the boathouse, he could almost feel her. He could swear he smelled her expensive scent hovering in the air like the haints the old people whispered about.

His hand brushed against something hard and cool—metal. He struggled to adjust his eyes to the thick darkness while his hands spread over the hood of a car. Cool already, its engine must have been off for a while.

"Sam?" Was she out there in the swamp alone? It was a dangerous place, with alligators and quicksand and sudden patches of deep water that could take you by surprise. "Sam!"

Panic ratcheted through his system, stoked by desire and painful longing. "Where are you?" He stood still, listening.

Patterns of sound played around him, rain on the leaves and grasses, and the hum of insects.

Louis.

His skin prickled with goose bumps. He could almost swear he heard someone call his name. He didn't actually hear it with his ears. He *felt* it.

Louis.

"I'm coming, Sam. Call out to me!" Urgency rang in his voice as he splashed around the boathouse and pulled the doors open. "Call for me, Sam. I'll find you."

Louis.

Again, he didn't hear her voice so much as feel it vibrate through him. "I'm coming for you, Sam. Keep calling." He didn't start the engine because it would drown out all sound. Instead he picked up the wooden paddle from the floor of the boat and started to row in the direction his instincts told him.

His muscles strained against the heavy, still water. He pushed the prow of the boat through the grasses thickening the dark, glistening surface as his whole being yearned and struggled toward Sam.

"Louis, I'm over here." At last her voice rose over the sound of raindrops. It was edged with desperation. He could hear her clear as a birdcall, about a hundred yards to his left.

In a split second he started the engine and chugged toward her. Moonlight picked out a slender female form, standing waist-high in tall grasses.

His heart leaped like a flying fish.

He cut the engine and paddled the last few yards, then reached out into the rain to grasp her hand in his. Powerful sensations surged through him as her fingers threaded through his, small and slippery with rain.

Her hair clung to her scalp and her flowered dress molded

to her slender body. A fierce wave of emotion crashed over him at the sight of her.

In a single, swift motion he seized her around the waist and tugged her into the boat, then found that he couldn't unlock his arms from around her, but kept clutching her closer and closer to his chest, although he had no idea why he was even here.

He didn't care why, as long as she *was* here.

Sobs racked her small frame. "Oh, Louis. I had to see you. I tried, I really did. I've been painting and everything, but nothing could stop me from…" Her voice rose to a high whine that cascaded into a shuddering sob.

"Shh." He put a finger to her quivering lips. "I've felt just the same. I can't get you out of my mind and it's driving me crazy." He pressed his cheek against her cool, wet one as feelings beyond words churned through him.

"Sorry."

Her wavering apology sent his chuckle rippling through both of them. "You should be. Driving us both half-mad when you knew all along that we're meant to be together."

Sam's eyes opened wide and stared into his. Rain and tears wet her lashes. "We are, aren't we? Meant to be together."

Fresh joy burst through him, so rich and sweet he couldn't help sassing her. "I could have told you that from day one. In fact, I think I did." He cocked his head. "But some people just won't listen to sense."

"And what you said, about having kids…" Her voice shook. "I might not be able to. I did try for three years with Larry and even though the tests didn't find anything, it's quite possible that—"

Louis crushed her to his chest. He couldn't stand to hear her doubt and fear, all of it so unnecessary.

"Then we'll adopt," he growled. "I'd love to welcome a child into our lives any way one is able to come. And you've already proved you can create a beautiful family from a group of confused and even angry strangers." He drew in a shuddering breath. "You're something else, Sam. You're really special and I'd be so honored and privileged to spend my life with you. Any child of yours will be the luckiest kid on earth."

Sam stared at him for a moment, water dripping from her nose and chin, then she let out a wail, something you might hear on an *I Love Lucy* episode when Ricky caught Lucy sneaking an expensive new hat into the house.

Louis burst into heartfelt laughter.

"But where will we live?" Panic flickered across her features. "You need to be in New Orleans, and to visit all your restaurants, but I need to be in New York most of the time to run the foundation. It isn't just a job I can pick up and leave. It's a huge responsibility that I take very seriously."

Louis struggled not to smile. She looked so very unprofessional with water soaking through her flowered dress and caressing the outlines of a flimsy-looking bra.

His voice emerged huskier than he intended. "We'll live like nomads, then."

"But what about the kids' schooling?" She swallowed. "I know it's a bit premature, but…"

"We'll homeschool them. My mom did that for me a lot of the time and I turned out okay. It'll be fun. They'll be at home wherever we go. Don't worry about trying to be 'normal' and to fit in with other people and their expectations. It's much more fun to just be *you*."

"You're right, of course." She inhaled and tucked a soggy strand of hair sheepishly behind her ears. "I've been painting."

"I know. Margo told me you're blowing people's minds

right, left and center. She thinks you're one of the major talents of the twenty-first century."

Sam blushed, even in the rain, and tried to wave her hand. "That ridiculous! They're just paintings. Representational. Totally unfashionable."

Louis just held her tighter, inhaling the rich, glorious scent of her and feeling for her warmth through her wet clothes. "Fashion means nothing when it comes to true beauty, Sam. That's what you have and what you create in the world around you. You've gotten lost a couple of times, and so have I…"

He drew in a breath as emotion threatened to choke him. "But I love you, Sam. And I know that as long as you and I stick together, we'll find our way somewhere wonderful."

Sam blinked at him, eyes glistening with hope and fear and so much more. "I love you, too, Louis. I tried not to, or at least not to love you in this way, but I couldn't help it."

She paused, and a smile flickered across her mouth. "And now I choose the road that leads into bed with you every night."

"We'd better make sure that bed has a roof over it, tonight." He looked up at the sky, dark with clouds spitting rain over the whole watery world. "I've got dry clothes at the cabin."

Mischief flickered in Sam's eyes. "I don't think we'll be needing those."

A jolt of lust shot straight to his groin. "I like the way you think."

He turned and tugged at the cord on the outboard motor and the engine grumbled to life. With one arm around Sam, Louis guided the boat through the familiar yet ever-changing waters.

To his favorite place, with his favorite person in the whole world.

* * * * *

"I'm the illegitimate daughter of notoriously scandalous parents, Mr. Milford. Candidates for my hand are unlikely to be lining up at the gates."

"Don't be so quick to discount your charms, my dear. Or the charm of your substantial dowry. Or even your brothers' influence. There are as many reasons to marry as there are marriages."

Annalise snorted. "Oh, yes. Perhaps I shall marry for dynastic reasons, or perhaps for property or influence. After all, a loveless, practical marriage worked out so well for my mother."

"Well, you've routed me on that one. I can think of no suitable rejoinder." Ned rose to his feet and extended his hand. "And since that is the case, let me be the first to wish you a long and happy spinsterhood."

Her mouth gaped open. And then she laughed.

And he froze.

This was the first time, Ned realized. The first time he'd seen her eyes light up and her mouth curl. The first time he'd witnessed her features melded together in glorious accord to produce exquisite beauty.

Unbelievable what a change came over her face. Unheard of what effect her throaty, rasping laughter had on his body. It pounded a beat upon his ear, quickly taken up by his pulse. It echoed through him, finally residing in his stirring nether regions.

So easily she did it, awakened these sensations within him—without any apparent effort at all. And she had called him potentially dangerous? Clearly the intelligent thing for him to do would be to steer clear, to leave her to the tender ministrations of Lord Peter Blackthorne.

"You were right." She smiled up at him as she took his hand and climbed to her feet. "I do feel better."

Ah, well. When had he ever chosen the intelligent path?

He did not relinquish her hand. He used it to pull her in, close enough that he could feel the warmth of her. "At the risk of repeating Lord Peter's mistake and anticipating too much— may I ask if you'll be my partner in battledore tomorrow?"

Her smile dimmed. Her breath came a little faster. His own had gone shallow, as if he'd just run a race—and lost. He ran his gaze over the appealing lift of her brow and the curious angle of her chin. His index finger twitched.

"I should like that," she said.

His finger trembled again and he lifted it, traced the pink and tender shell of her ear, the unique sweep of her jaw. Her pulse leaped beneath her skin, triggering his own. Slowly he tilted her chin up, waiting for her to object, to step back, to slap his hand away.

She did none of those eminently sensible things. Which left him free to do the entirely impractical thing.

Baby soft, the skin of her lips. Her whole body trembled when he touched her there.

He leaned in. Her eyes closed, even as she stood straight against him, strung as tight as a bow. He pressed his mouth to hers. It was a soft kiss, sweet and chaste. And yet he was hot and hard and as ready as he'd ever been in his life.

She drew back a little. Sighed. Their breath mingled a moment before she slowly backed away.

"Oh," she breathed. Her dark eyes were full of wonder and something that looked like fear. He took a step toward her, but she only shook her head. His outstretched hand fell to his side as she turned to disappear into the wood. This was the first time, Ned realized. The first time, since he'd come to the house party at Welbourne Manor, that he'd seen her eyes light up.

* * * * *

Follow Ned and Annalise's story in May 2009 in
THE DIAMONDS OF WELBOURNE MANOR
Available May 2009 from Harlequin® Historical

Available in the series romance section,
or in the historical romance section,
wherever books are sold.

**We'll be spotlighting a different series
every month throughout 2009
to celebrate our 60th anniversary.**

Look for Harlequin® Historical in May!

Celebrations begin with
a sumptuous Regency house party!

Join three scandalous sisters in

THE DIAMONDS OF
WELBOURNE MANOR

Glittering, scintillating, sensual fun
by Diane Gaston, Deb Marlowe
and Amanda McCabe.

**60 years of Harlequin,
600 years of romance
in Harlequin Historical!**

REQUEST YOUR FREE BOOKS!

2 FREE NOVELS PLUS 2 FREE GIFTS!

Passionate, Powerful, Provocative!

YES! Please send me 2 FREE Silhouette Desire® novels and my 2 FREE gifts (gifts are worth about $10). After receiving them, if I don't wish to receive any more books, I can return the shipping statement marked "cancel". If I don't cancel, I will receive 6 brand-new novels every month and be billed just $4.05 per book in the U.S. or $4.74 per book in Canada. That's a savings of almost 15% off the cover price! It's quite a bargain! Shipping and handling is just 25¢ per book*. I understand that accepting the 2 free books and gifts places me under no obligation to buy anything. I can always return a shipment and cancel at any time. Even if I never buy another book, the two free books and gifts are mine to keep forever.

225 SDN ERVX 326 SDN ERVM

Name	(PLEASE PRINT)
Address	Apt. #
City	State/Prov.	Zip/Postal Code

Signature (if under 18, a parent or guardian must sign)

Mail to the Silhouette Reader Service:
IN U.S.A.: P.O. Box 1867, Buffalo, NY 14240-1867
IN CANADA: P.O. Box 609, Fort Erie, Ontario L2A 5X3

Not valid to current subscribers of Silhouette Desire books.

Want to try two free books from another line?
Call 1-800-873-8635 or visit www.morefreebooks.com.

* Terms and prices subject to change without notice. Prices do not include applicable taxes. Sales tax applicable in N.Y. Canadian residents will be charged applicable provincial taxes and GST. Offer not valid in Quebec. This offer is limited to one order per household. All orders subject to approval. Credit or debit balances in a customer's account(s) may be offset by any other outstanding balance owed by or to the customer. Please allow 4 to 6 weeks for delivery. Offer available while quantities last.

Your Privacy: Silhouette Books is committed to protecting your privacy. Our Privacy Policy is available online at www.eHarlequin.com or upon request from the Reader Service. From time to time we make our lists of customers available to reputable third parties who may have a product or service of interest to you. If you would prefer we not share your name and address, please check here. ☐

SDES09

You're invited to join our Tell Harlequin Reader Panel!

By joining our new reader panel you will:

- Receive Harlequin® books—they are FREE and yours to keep with no obligation to purchase anything!
- Participate in fun online surveys
- Exchange opinions and ideas with women just like you
- Have a say in our new book ideas and help us publish the best in women's fiction

In addition, you will have a chance to win great prizes and receive special gifts! See Web site for details. Some conditions apply. Space is limited.

To join, visit us at

www.TellHarlequin.com.

COMING NEXT MONTH
Available May 12, 2009

#1939 BILLIONAIRE EXTRAORDINAIRE—Leanne Banks
Man of the Month
Determined to get revenge on his enemy, he convinces his
buttoned-up new assistant to give him the information he needs—
by getting her to *un*button a few things….

**#1940 PROPOSITIONED INTO A FOREIGN AFFAIR—
Catherine Mann**
The Hudsons of Beverly Hills
A fling in France with a Hollywood starlet turns into a calculated
affair in L.A. But is she really the only woman sharing his bed?

#1941 MONTANA MISTRESS—Sara Orwig
Stetsons & CEOs
It's an offer she finds hard to refuse: he'll buy her family's hotel—
if she'll be his mistress for a month.

#1942 THE ONCE AND FUTURE PRINCE—Olivia Gates
The Castaldini Crown
There is only one woman who can convince this prince to take the
throne. And there is only one way he'll ever agree—by reigniting
their steamy love affair.

**#1943 THE MORETTI ARRANGEMENT—
Katherine Garbera**
Moretti's Legacy
When he discovers his assistant has been selling company secrets,
he decides to keep a closer eye on her…clothing optional!

#1944 THE TYCOON'S REBEL BRIDE—Maya Banks
The Anetakis Tycoons
She arrives in town determined to get her man at any cost. But
suddenly it isn't clear anymore who is seducing whom….

SDCNMBPA0409